CAPTIVE DESIRE

WILLOW WINTERS

From *USA Today* bestselling romance author
Willow Winters comes an unexpectedly hot
stand-alone with two Alphas and one human mate.
Get ready for a fast paced and steamy paranormal
novella in the To Be Claimed world that romance
readers can't stop raving about.

We tracked her down, now we're keeping her.
After all she's our mate...

We're the twin Alphas of Dark Valley, opposite in
almost every way but both of us are shocked that
we share a mate...and that she's human. I have no
idea how this pretty little woman could handle one
of us, let alone both. When lust turns to obsession,
neither of us will be able to fight the pull to her and
I'm not sure either of us will be willing to share.

She never could have known what searching for
answers about shifters could lead to and neither
could we. Now the only thing she'll be learning is
who she belongs to.

If you enjoy sexy, Alpha werewolves and stand-
alone, insta-love stories, complete with a happily
ever after, this book is for you.

CAPTIVE DESIRE

PROLOGUE

Emma

"UGH!" I GROAN, SLEEP STILL HEAVILY pulling me under as the alarm goes off. I feel like I'd just gotten to sleep and my discontent is muffled into the pillow. My bed is snug and warm, and the air is so cold that I really, *really* don't want to get out of my comfy cocoon.

Beep, beep, beep.

I lazily pick up the handheld device so hell-bent on yelling at me and hit snooze by accident. Gritting my teeth, I toss it on the nightstand. My head hits the pillow and I almost let sleep pull me back under, but then I remember what day it is. Instantly, my mind wakes with excitement.

I've waited *years* for a lead and I finally got one. Wasting no time on the wish for sleep, I race to my closet and grab the first pair of jeans and tank top I can get my hands on. There are at least two were-wolves hunting on land only an hour away from here according to a reputable source. I squeal internally as I dig in the pile of shoes for the only pair of sneakers I own. I'm going to need them so I can hunt down these shifters.

The alarm goes off again while I'm grabbing my toothbrush and I don't mind the relentless beeping in the least. I smile as I turn it off and slip my phone into my back pocket. The only other object on my nightstand is an empty picture frame and looking at it makes my smile slip. My boss and the head of *The Daily Tribune* gave it to me for Christmas. I was going to put a picture of my parents in it, but that's too damn depressing to have to look at first thing in the morning. I cringe and lay the frame flat. I'll get back to that later. I have other things to focus on today. Hopefully much happier things that require my attention.

I've been working on this petition for nearly a

year. It's something my parents felt strongly about as well, and that alarming offering at Shadow Falls screwed everything up for me. I know there's far more to the werewolves than the Authority lets on. And now everyone's convinced that shifters are nothing but vicious beasts who take whatever and whoever they want and do God knows what with them. The rebellion is growing, and my petition has lost its following. No one wants to combine our worlds. They want the shifters and other paranormal beings to have even less access. Ideally none at all.

It's a shame that a single incident could cause such an uproar and put all of my work into question. But I'm going to prove that werewolves are just like us. Well more like us than we're led to believe.

It's not hard to imagine the beasts with their broad shoulders and towering frames. They're the epitome of lust and power. Forbidden and dangerous and therefore the most delightful temptation. Their dark eyes haunt me in the most delicious way. I've seen the way they touch the women and imagined myself on the stage. Being chosen. Offered, taken, and claimed. My core heats as the fantasy plays in my head. I snap my eyes open and cringe. I really need to get more AA batteries. My poor BOB (battery operated boyfriend) must be missing me. Silently laughing and then cringing at my joke, I have to admit how depressing my social life has become. Besides, I have been offered before and I wasn't chosen. It's a sad truth, but I'm not meant to belong to them. It doesn't mean we can't share the same world though.

I grab my keys and my backpack. Taking one last look at my nearly empty loft, I close the door and pray I can catch up to the werewolves. I need to record something, *anything*, to convince the world that the division we've created is causing more harm than good.

CHAPTER ONE

WITH THE TIP I'VE BEEN GIVEN, I'M almost certain I'm close to the pack, or at least to the two werewolves I've been tracking. My boots certainly have enough mud on them, and my legs are sore from all the hiking. At this point I think they want me to catch up to them. I've been following their footprints through the woods for almost two days now, taking me farther and farther out into the wilderness. I grew up camping and hiking; my parents loved it. But the first night felt different. I've spent nearly a year shoving all emotion down, but the farther I get out here, alone with my thoughts, the more difficult it is to keep everything buried. So I follow the trail relentlessly. I need to find them. I have no other option.

The werewolves' prints are similar to wolves' but much, *much* larger. All this morning I started to worry I was wrong and that they were only the marks of abnormally large wolves, but then I saw the change and human footprints replaced the paws. Watching the transition was electrifying. It's hard to explain the rush of emotion knowing how close I am to them. Is it against the law? Yes. Did that keep me from documenting it? Hell no. It lit a fire under my ass to catch up to them when I saw those prints. It's odd enough that there are only two of them. I expected to see more prints by now since loners are a rarity. *Supposedly*. At least that's what my research has hinted at.

I should've headed back yesterday as soon as it got dark. It's not like I'm really prepared to be out here on my own, but I've got a few power bars, another two bottles of water, and a blanket in my backpack. I'll deal with it. All I really need is something to sleep on and something to eat. Not that I slept much last night. How could I when I'm so damn close to them?

The scout that led me here is probably shitting his pants thinking I've died. There's no one who could sue him if I died on his land though, so he'll be fine. I should've called him yesterday when I had a signal and told him that I found tracks and was going to follow them. I doubt he'll come search for me. It may be his land, but he's not a fool. The shifters have been hunting here, and he has no intention of coming between a wolf and his prey. I might believe we shouldn't be separated, but not everyone thinks that way. Most people don't. Because we don't know enough.

My career is finally going to take off once I get video evidence to back up my data. I've been studying werewolves for years, but it's always been received with heavy skepticism. I'm the most widely talked about journalist and researcher, and definitely respected by many, but with all of the false information out there…well, at this point I need proof to take me to the next level.

I'm willing to do whatever I need to in order to get this story. This is the chance I've been waiting for and I'm not going to back down for anything.

The Authority knows I want an interview and to stay among the werewolves. Their PR response that it would be unsafe for both species still enrages me. I wouldn't have to be out here tracking prints like a hunter if they would have simply given me any contact whatsoever. Just a chance. That's all I wanted. I've seen werewolves at the offerings, I've listened to them and their *mates*. It's so obvious to me. It's enraging that no one believes me. Humans want to believe the worst of them, and with all the propaganda and unfortunate history, it's easy enough to simply believe what's been fed to us. But I know the truth and I'm going to film it. I want to see a werewolf with a human mate. I know they exist. I know it in the core of my soul. Then they'll take me seriously and my petition to merge our worlds could possibly gain some traction. If the Authority doesn't like it, they can shove it up their asses.

The two sets of large paw prints are closer together as I near the small clearing in the woods. No longer distance between the prints that indicates large steps, they're now merely inches apart and twist in the dirt, becoming a confusing mess. My gaze narrows as I try to differentiate the paths of the two wolves. The dark forest is bathed in filters of light as I follow their messy trail.

The scent of woods is intoxicating and the fresh air is cool against my skin. I take a moment to steady my breathing and then try to make out what exactly they were doing.

They slowed down nearly to a stop right about here, right at the entrance to the small clearing. That makes me nervous. It takes everything in me not to touch the prints. Something feels off. For the first time since I began, it feels unsettling. It's only been about an hour since the sun rose and I found where they slept last night. They didn't slow to eat or drink. They slept by the river, so I imagine they drank and ate there. The only other reason I can think for them to slow their approach at this clearing is because there was something here that made them stall. Other shifters maybe? Vampires?

The thought makes my blood run cold and my breath stalls in my lungs. Werewolves I'm familiar with, but other species? No. I don't know much about other species other than what we're told, and even though I don't believe much of it, it doesn't stop me from thinking the worst right now. I don't know how to avoid conflict with any other supernatural beings. Werewolves are easy, simple submission is all they require, and I intend to submit once I finally reach them.

I don't want to give them any reason to send me away, or worse. I only want a chance to stay with them and learn more about them. *And film them.* But they don't need to know about that.

Cautiously, I follow the prints in the damp dirt, pushing dried leaves and pesky sticks out of my way so I can be sure not to lose the trail of their casual strides. Just as I get to the edge of the tree line, the prints split with one wolf going right and the other going left. Initially, I feel a bit of relief. They wouldn't split up if there was any kind of danger nearby.

Swallowing thickly, I stare at the tracks and look deeper into the woods where the set of tracks on the right leads. I'm vaguely familiar with the area. I studied the map that Jordan, the scout and owner of the land, gave me. My forehead pinches in confusion. There's nothing but woods that way and then a cliff that drops to nothing. I look to the left and then drop my bag at my feet so I can take out the map. To the left is Shadow Falls, and no shifter would go that way. That area is claimed by a ruthless pack. I watched their offering. I was there and saw the women's reaction to being taken. Chills flow down my spine at the memory. They're the reason no one believes me about them only taking mates. I huff and loosen the hair tie to take down my hair, running my hand through my brunette locks as I study the map. I'm certain my hair is a mess, my worn jeans have dirt stains on my knees, and my sweatshirt is less than fresh after two days of hiking in it. I take a moment to slip it off, leaving me in my tank top. It's warm enough that I can have a moment to feel the fresh air and maybe get some warmth from the sun on my skin. The sounds of nature pause, and it forces me to look up. It's practically silent. No more birds chirping or critters rustling. My heart rate picks up, but I glance back down to the map, knowing exactly what I've done and what the risks are.

There's a small stream and Dark Valley between here and Shadow Falls, but I can't imagine why the wolves would split at this point.

My hand is still in my hair, I'm frozen with fear and my entire body shivers at the sound of a branch cracking beneath a heavy weight behind me. And then another. They're casual steps, definitely getting closer and getting louder, more careless. *The wolves.* My breath comes in short pants and my eyes widen. Another noise to my right forces a small gasp of fear from me.

They split up to trap me.

I don't turn around. I know better than to do that. I can handle this. I calm myself by breathing as slowly as possible and gently lowering my body to the ground. My heart only speeds up as the sounds get closer. I can do this. This is what I've wanted for so long. To come face to face with the werewolves.

Adrenaline spikes through my body making my heart race and beat chaotically. My hands are numb with fear. My instincts tell me to run, but I know better than to do that. I gently place my palms on the dirt and push them forward to lower my body into a bow even though I'm facing away from both of the wolves moving behind me. The smell of dirt and grass helps me relax slightly as the sounds of several heavy steps get louder and louder.

My shoulders and chest rise as I breathe heavily, struggling to remain calm. My eyes refuse to close, and I find myself staring toward the open field, where the only bit of light is illuminating the forest. I swallow thickly as both wolves move only feet from me. Their presence and dominance are an overwhelming physical force pressing against me. Regret passes through me as my anxiety rises. Everything in me wants to run as the fear of the unknown races through me, but I stay strong. I'm doing this for a righteous cause. I'm confident in my work. I hold on to the last bit of strength that I have and do my best to just breathe and wait for the werewolves to give me their consent to rise.

My body tenses and trembles on the cold, hard ground as I sense a large form on my left. The warm breath of the wolf sends a chill of goosebumps down my neck. His jaws are close to my neck; warning me, daring me. This is the test I knew they'd present to me. The knowledge that I was right in what their initial reaction would be makes me feel slightly at ease, even if his jaws are within an inch of my throat and large enough to rip into my flesh and end my life in an instant.

The heat sends an immediate spike of desire through me, making me clench my thighs and repress a moan. The craving is at odds with the terror that's natural to feel in the presence of wolves. I cling to it in order to suppress my need to run away from the danger. The wolf scents the air and a low rumble of approval growls in the small space between us, making my body heat and my clit throb.

Yet again, the physical force of their presence is undeniable and shocking. I shouldn't feel this way. It's wrong. I know it is. And yet…

The other wolf approaches and pushes my simple tank top up my back with his nose, exposing my skin.

The cold, wet feeling on my sensitized skin makes my body shudder, but I do my best to keep still. It's important to make it clear that I have no intention to challenge them. I keep repeating that very important fact in my head while I tilt my head slightly, exposing more of my neck. I want to make my submission obvious. I'm at their mercy. My heart pounds in my chest as a large white paw steps just a mere inch in front of my face. The pads dig into the dirt and remain planted in front of me as the wolf lowers his head to my cheek, scenting me.

I want to close my eyes and hide, but the fear of death is keeping them wide open. My heart hammers against my rib cage as his breath tickles my neck. A low growl from the other wolf has a whimper falling from my lips without my consent and my hands fist in a weak attempt to cower. I immediately flatten them again. My breath stops short as a vicious snarl erupts from my left.

Fuck!

I should've never fisted my hands. Fuck, fuck, fuck! I part my lips ready to plead with the wolves, but the second I open my mouth the paw leaves my vision with a heavy sound of the massive beast stepping over my body and leaving me in my passive position alone. I stay still waiting to hear what they're doing. I know they must only be feet from me, but I can't hear them moving. Are they waiting for me? Are they testing me? I've never considered much of what's expected of me past this point. I didn't plan on it being this intense, this terrifying. My eyes dart frantically from the clearing to the trees, waiting anxiously for any sign from the wolves as to what I should do. My neck remains stiff from the fear and my knees ache to move.

Everything in me begs me to lift my head and see them, but I'm too fucking scared. My body is paralyzed. I need to gather the strength to approach them. I knew this would happen and I planned on it. I was so eager to catch up to them. But actually being near them, I wasn't prepared to feel their power. I wasn't prepared to be so afraid. After a long moment of almost silence, shuffling occurs a few feet from me. Leaves are scattered in my periphery followed by a loud huff from the snout of one of the massive shifters. The air around me moves as the sound of the wolf stalking toward me gets louder. My body trembles and I wait with bated breath, hoping they'll give me a chance to speak.

Then the sound changes. No longer the pounding

of heavy paws on the ground. Instead it's the sound of a man walking with confidence and taking determined strides. It's softer, yet just as intimidating.

He shifted.

The knowledge brings me hope that I'll be able to follow through with my plan and find the courage to speak. I try to lift my head again, but I'm still frozen in place. My body is incapable of moving in the presence of such dominance. My breath picks up as he walks past my head, stopping at my side to tower over me.

In this moment there are only two things I am sure of. A naked shifter is hovering over my bowed body, deciding what he wants to do with me. And I am completely at his mercy.

My body jolts as a large, strong hand settles on my lower back. A low growl erupts from him as I move instinctually against his touch. I didn't mean to, but my body reacts on its own accord and tries to escape his hold. His other hand splays across my shoulder blades and pushes my upper half back onto the ground. The firm shove doesn't hurt, but his power over me is evident. His desire for me to remain submissive has been made clear. I press my lips together and pray for his compassion.

It's a heady feeling to be at the mercy of someone

who possesses so much strength. Someone who could ruin you without much thought or energy. My blood heats as his hands slowly move, lessening in pressure and traveling leisurely over my body. His fingers barely graze my skin and send tingles of want through me. His touch makes me writhe faintly beneath him. I resist the urge as best I can and concentrate on keeping my breath even.

A short, low groan vibrates in the air as his hands leave my body. I finally lift my head and dare to look at him. I slowly rise on all fours, waiting to feel the shifter's hands on me again. I keep my head bowed, but he allows me to raise my head and chest off the ground with no objection.

A white wolf with piercing blue eyes within my arm's reach watches my movements but doesn't protest them. He stands tall scrutinizing me with an unyielding gaze. My lips part at his beauty and the obvious strength he possesses. His massive body stands out against the forest with dominance; the very nature surrounding us is bowing to him. His eyes are cold and hard, watching me as though he's waiting to pounce on his prey. The sight of him makes my breath hitch and blood scorch.

A movement to my left makes my eyes dart to the

shifter standing over me. My eyes widen as I take in the vision of the broad-shouldered man, his tanned skin taut over hard muscle. His thick, black hair falls wildly just before his shoulders, his silver eyes heat as I meet his curious gaze. I feel an intense pull to bow to him, to lower myself back to the ground and wait for his orders. Dark stubble lines his masculine jaw as a small, sexy grin slips into place. He's pleased by my reaction. A purr of satisfaction vibrates through me, as though his approval is all that's necessary.

Between the two beasts, I'm not sure which is the Alpha, they both have an air to them that demands obedience. But there's no question that they could both destroy me.

The werewolf's grin morphs into a cocky smirk as his eyes roam my body. "Come." He speaks his command in a low, masculine tone as he turns his back to me and walks away, leaving me to stare at the corded muscles in his arms and legs and his bare ass that has my pussy aching with need. He's confident that I'll follow him. And he's right. My mouth opens to speak, but immediately I slam my jaw shut. I can't question him or his authority.

I move to my knees and ready my still-shaking body to obey him, but as my eyes reach the wolf's gaze ahead of me, I still. I'm afraid to even breathe too loud as the intense stare from the wolf entraps me. My body chills as he continues to glare at me, as if daring me to follow him. I feel trapped between the two of them. One commanding me to follow and the other warning me to stay away. It's not until the other shifter passes the wolf that the beast turns to move deeper into the forest, releasing me to make my decision.

CHAPTER TWO

Owen

IT TAKES TOO FUCKING LONG FOR HER TO GET her sweet ass up off the ground and follow us. I glance to my left and glare at Luke. "Knock it the fuck off." I scold him in my head, but he still doesn't turn away from her. "What the fuck is your problem?" I don't understand why he's so pissed off. He should be grateful. "Aren't you happy we have her now?"

"She's human." His low voice echoes in my head as he turns away from her and starts to walk with me, deeper into the forest and closer to home. We still have two days until we'll be back to our pack, and I can't fucking wait to get our mate into bed.

Our mate.

"Obviously." My chest aches thinking we may never have come across our mate had we not stopped to see who was trailing us.

"She's weak." He practically snarls the words, and I stop in my tracks to stare him down. My fists clench and my nostrils flare in anger. I hear her steps come to a halt behind me and smell her fear. *Shit.* She thinks my anger for her, as though she's done something to disappoint me. I snort at the thought and relax my posture for her peace of mind. Her submission was perfect; there's not a single thing she did to make me angry. She knew exactly how to behave, and it was a damn beautiful sight to see someone so stunning and vulnerable carry themselves with courage and confidence. She's at least a foot shorter than both of us and there's no way she'd be able to keep us off her, but she had the bravery not to run and the wisdom not to challenge us. Weak isn't a word I'd use to describe her, and it infuriates me that Luke thinks so little of her.

Our mate has yet to move, and the smell of her distress makes my gut twist and my wolf whine. Her breathing comes in short, panicked pants and it's a fucking sexy sound, but I hate that it's caused by fear. Especially fear of me. My fingers itch to comfort her. I shift, reveling in the feel of my joints stretching and the burn of my muscles morphing to fit the beast I am. Our little mate takes a hesitant step back as I turn to face her in wolf form.

She's fucking gorgeous. She's curvy, but somehow still athletic in build. Her dark hair nearly hits her waist. Without a second look, one may think she's plain because of the simple clothes she wears, but her natural features reflect nothing but beauty. Her sweet vanilla smell fills my lungs. Her dark eyes captivate me and her pale, plump lips tempt me to take them with my own. The smell of her sweet arousal nearly has me pushing her down and fucking her in the dirt.

Desire stirs inside of me as I remember how she pushed against me, as though she'd fight me. I love her submissive behavior, but it was rehearsed. I can't wait to put it to the test and I fucking hope she does fight me…that she would enjoy pushing my boundaries and I could do the same with her. I could prove my dominance to her in a way we'd both enjoy.

I can just imagine what it would've been like to have my way with her, licking across her collarbone and up to her ear. I bet she tastes as sweet as she smells. And if she struggled against me, like she did initially… I repress my groan of pleasure. I'd enjoy it far too much. I'd push her knees apart, spread her legs wide with my hips and fuck her into the dirt like an animal. With her sweet scent in the air, I know that pussy has to be slick and wet for me. I could thrust easily into her welcoming heat and feel her tight, hot walls pulse around my thick cock as she comes. At least then I would've been able to take this edge off.

The pull to her is undeniable. And judging by her scent, she feels something for me as well. I've known of mates and fated bonds all my life, but this is something I could have never prepared for.

I've never felt this need for someone. Not just a need to fuck her, but a need to be her everything. A need to live for her. She's the only one who matters now.

Not even my twin.

The undeserving prick who glares at our mate simply because she's human. He's an idiot and a liar if he says he doesn't want to claim her beautiful ass as much as I do. I've never felt this pull and desire to possess like I do with her. She did this to me. She's awoken something deep in my soul. She woke a savage part of the beast inside me.

I'm on edge and itching with need. I'll only calm down once I take her as my beast demands. I pace around my mate, watching as she attempts to lower herself again. I move closer to lie on the ground beside her and wait for her to realize I want her to ride me. I'll be able to get her home that much faster without the need to slow to her pace, and then she can really ride me. A satisfied rumble in my chest fills me with warmth.

"I want her first." Luke's voice breaks through the intoxicating thought I have of her delectable mouth, sucking every bit of lust I have for her out of me. I have to hold back the growl growing inside of me. I've always shared everything with my twin and I know I'll have to share her, but the thought of giving him access to her when he doesn't hold her with the respect he should pisses me off.

"You said she was weak."

"She is." His blunt statement puts me even further on edge. It's been years since we fought, but I'm more than ready to tear into him if he keeps up this attitude. Between the two of us, I'm the peacekeeper, the one who keeps things light around the pack. Luke is too dark and intense and too much of a hothead. I grunt a response to him as our mate slowly spears her fingers through my black fur, finding her confidence again now that she's sure I'm not angry with her. I love the feel of her hands on me. She lets out a surprised squeak as Luke pushes his nose against her ass to get her on top of me. "And I'm not sure I want to wait until we get back." His words barely register with me as she settles on top of me and grips my fur in her tiny fists. "I can smell her heat."

She doesn't know it yet, but soon enough she'll know exactly who she belongs to. She belongs to us. The Alphas of Dark Valley.

CHAPTER THREE

Emma

AFTER HOURS OF HOLDING ON, I'M SO tired and my hands and thighs are killing me from gripping onto the wolf. My muscles are sore from straining for the hours that I've been on his back and my entire body is stinging from holding on with every jolt as the two werewolves raced through the forest. I think they enjoyed my reaction when they barreled through the trees and ducked under branches. My heavy breathing and tight grip on him only seemed to motivate the wolf to move harder and faster.

If I'm honest, it's exhilarating. I can't imagine

anyone else has ever gotten to feel this before. Maybe their mates, the women they've chosen at offerings. My heart races yet again and I know I need to speak up the first chance I'm given. I have no idea where we're going or what the shifters want with me, but I need them to know what I want.

It's nearly pitch black out now and we've slowed down. The only light we have shines down from the crescent moon. I'm not sure what's going on or where they're taking me. We moved so fast that I lost track of where we are. I don't think I could get home now even if I wanted to. Logically, I know I should be scared about the fact that I'm stranded and at their mercy, but instead I feel calm and protected. Maybe that makes me stupid, but at the moment I don't seem to mind.

The noises of the night silence as we enter a small cave in the side of the mountain. It can barely fit both wolves, but they settle down and get comfortable, shifting their weight slightly. I'm finally given a moment to lift my body off the black wolf. I take a moment to stretch my sore muscles and rehearse in my head what I need to say first, though the ache of my body takes all my attention. Even my eyes are sore. I close my eyes, enjoying the free movement of my body.

My heart jumps up into my throat and I scream as the black wolf's teeth nip my hip. I throw my body off the wolf and hit my back hard against the jagged rock, shoving my small frame between the massive beast and the unmoving wall.

A snarl rips through the small cave, echoing off the walls. It's then that I really take the situation for what it is. My heart races and my breath staggers as my back scrapes against the rock behind me. The wolves don't seem to pay any attention to my reaction, instead they engage in a silent discussion. I recognize the way they look at each other and the small movements that mirror conversations. I part my lips to speak, but the white wolf stares back at me, silencing me before I've even uttered a word.

I press my lips together and restrain myself from cowering. If they intended to harm me, they would've done so already. The black wolf acts as a barrier between me and the white wolf. I feel safe with him between the two of us. Something about the white wolf makes me feel uneasy. My skin tingles and heats looking at him. Waiting for him. That's the feeling that's overwhelming me. I'm waiting for him to make a decision. And I have a bad feeling that when he does, I'm never going to be the same.

Just as I come to that realization, my protector stands and leaves the cave, freeing the space between me and the white wolf. I stand still against the wall, holding my breath as the tips of my fingers dig into the rock behind me. It's only for a moment though. The other wolf returns and nudges me with his snout to the center of the cave, pushing me closer to the white wolf, exactly where I don't want to be.

He's obviously displeased with my hesitation and reluctance to be close to him. He lowers his body to the ground and closes his eyes, suddenly disinterested in my presence. I don't feel any sense of relief though. The black wolf does the same behind me, lying low to the ground and resting. The two massive wolves come up past my hips while I'm standing, but being surrounded by the two of them is both exhilarating and intimidating. I'm left standing between the two, trapped in the small cave.

A moment passes and the chill of the night creeps through the thin tank top. My eyes search for the backpack, but I must've dropped it when I was startled earlier. Panic sets in. I could climb over the black wolf and dig between him and the wall, but I'm not sure how well that action would be received. I also don't want to turn my back on the white wolf.

I could speak, but I'm terrified to push boundaries. I'm not sure what the protocol is, but I know that when they're ready to speak with me they will and if I'm smart, I'll keep my mouth shut until then.

I settle down between the two mammoth beasts and just like earlier, there's a pressure, a force I've never felt before. I immediately feel relaxed surrounded by their warmth. A sense of peace settles in my chest as I push my back snuggly against the thick fur of the black wolf. It's heady like a drug. It's undeniable that my control drifts from me. I'm conscious of it and yet I don't mind. I wish I had my recorder, I pray I don't forget this feeling. It's nearly magical. A masculine woodsy smell fills the air and I breathe it in, loving the scent. A small sigh leaves my lips as my heavy lids close. They open slightly as the wolves shift around me getting themselves comfortable, closing me in even more. As they settle, I drift off, feeling my body lighten and my breathing even and submit to the need to sleep.

A slight chill makes my shoulders hunch and my hands search for my blanket. I slowly part my eyes, waking from the deep sleep and remember the day before.

The shifters.

My body nearly jackknifes off the ground as I search the cave for the wolves. With my heart racing, I realize I'm alone. My backpack is in the very back of the cave, left opened. But other than that, the cave is empty. My heart sinks and my body numbs with a sickening feeling that they've left me.

They've gone. I had them here with me and I didn't say a damn word. I didn't get a single recording.

Tears prick at my eyes as my fists clench. My heart shatters and the sadness surprises me. I've always wanted this, but the strong reaction is unwanted and not something I'm used to. I can't even remember the last time I've cried. I have no idea why I'm feeling such intense emotions, such sadness. It's illogical. I don't understand and yet I can't control it. A noise at the entrance of the cave makes me tense.

Although his hair is blond, in the same wild style as the other shifter, he has a darkness about him. The way he carries his weight is as though he's stalking a prey. Hunting something. A lump grows in my throat as he approaches me without taking his striking blue eyes off me. My eyes widen as they travel down his muscular body. His massive dick is so hard, it barely moves as he walks, standing straight up. My bottom lip drops open in both shock and awe. He palms his cock and chuckles, making me realize that I'm staring. A hot blush travels up my chest and into my cheeks. I lower my gaze to the ground although I can still track his movements in my periphery. He stops right in front of me, lies on the ground, and then props up on his elbows. The heat from his body radiates toward me. The sight of his muscular frame sends a shiver of need through me, heating my core.

I'm ashamed by my reaction. I know wolves don't react this way. They only have urges for their mates. Yet here I am, turned on by both shifters and aching with the need to be touched by both of them. I close my eyes and try to will the thoughts away. I'm only here for research.

I can't cave to a primitive desire, though I've never felt this need before. I've never allowed myself to get close enough to a man, let alone had any of the feelings that devastate me in the presence of the werewolves. Just as I push my feelings aside, the shifter speaks. Startling me with his low, baritone command. "Suck."

My eyes shoot to his in shock as he strokes

himself. I watch his large hand grip his cock and slowly wrap around the top, spreading the precum around his head. My mouth waters at the sight, and my entire body wants to pounce at the invitation to take him into my mouth. But I can't believe what I've heard. This goes against everything I know. I stare back at him in disbelief.

His eyes narrow and an urge to bow to him pushes me to the ground. The heavy weight shoots a sharp pain through my body, making me wince and moan beneath him. In an instant the feelings are gone and his large, rough hand cups my chin, tilting my head to look at him. His eyes search mine for a moment, and I have no idea what to do other than to look back into his icy blue gaze. A moment passes between us. His eyes pierce into mine and my heart pounds over and over again. My body warms at his touch. Instead of fear, I feel warmth and comfort. I feel a longing I can't explain. There's an intense pull of lust and desire.

His thumb rests against my lower lip before pushing into my mouth. I easily part for him and gently suck. A low groan of approval reverberates off the walls. I close my eyes, enjoying the taste of him in my mouth and feel encouraged with his approval. He pulls his hand away far too soon and I immediately miss his touch. He strokes himself again, just inches from my lowered body.

His hand fists the hair at the base of my neck and he gently pulls me toward him. The slight pain is directly linked to the throbbing need in my now-soaked pussy. Everything about him seems forbidden and mysterious. It's so fucking hot. His half-hooded eyes follow my tongue as I lick my lips. I've never done anything like this. I've never wanted to, either. But looking between his heated gaze and his massive cock, I can't help the lust heating every inch of me. I whimper in need, clenching my thighs.

What's wrong with me? I'm only vaguely conscious of how it's all unfolded. Something's not right and yet in this moment, all I need is him.

His grip on me loosens as I lower my lips to his dick. I take a languid lick of his rigid cock before taking the head in my mouth. It's difficult to do, but I relax my jaw and ease him in with my lips shielding my teeth. He's far too big for me to get much of him in my mouth, but I work his shaft with my hand as I obey him and suck and swallow as much as I can. I may not have experience, but I'm not that naïve. I know what he wants and I'm more than willing to give it to him.

The taste of his precum is salty and sweet. I release his dick with a pop and lick the head, dipping the tip of my tongue into his seam at the top. His leg twitches at the act and a low, strangled groan leaves his lips. My cheeks heat as I blush.

This is really happening. My heart races.

His intense blue eyes stare back at me with lust, and his full lips are parted as his breath leaves him in shallow pants. I feel scandalous to be doing such an act. But I love the power it gives me to see that I can have a man of such authority and dominance lost in the pleasure I give him. I moan around his cock as his hand gently caresses my neck. He's letting me go at my own pace as I move up and down his length.

I close my eyes, enjoying the taste of him, the sounds of desire, the feel of his hands on me. It's surreal that I'm doing this. Especially with *him*. A werewolf. Shame hits me as I realize I don't even know his name. The recognition wakes me from the lust-filled haze. I instantly let go of him and push away, covering my swollen lips with my hand, scooting back in the dirt on my ass until my back is pushed against the hard rock. What the fuck is wrong with me? His eyes widen and flash with a hint of anger, making me instinctually recoil.

When he sees my reaction he schools his features. He looks down at his still-hard dick and then back at me with confusion. "Did I hurt you?" I slowly shake my head, wondering how he thought he hurt me. "Why have you stopped?"

"I—" I look down at my dirty jeans and stutter. My cheeks flame with embarrassment. "I don't even know your name."

"Luke." His statement comes out hard and he's obviously still confused. "You're Emma." How does he know my name? As if reading my mind, he answers, "I went through your things."

Oh. I suppose it's good that he at least knows my name. I attempt to give him a small smile, but I fail. Instead tears burn my eyes, threatening to reveal themselves and I have no idea why. I'm so confused and I feel lost. This isn't what I wanted and it's nothing like what I'd planned. A thick lump grows in my throat, and my chest hurts so much I have to push my hand against it in hope of relieving some of the pressure.

"There's something wrong with me. I want to go home." I can hardly believe my own words. They come out without my consent. I've wanted the chance to speak openly to werewolves for as long as I can remember, but I've lost the courage. I can't find it in me to even look back at the shifter.

"We'll be home tomorrow." My eyes widen and dart to his, and I start frantically shaking my head.

"No I need to go back home. To my home. I can't do this." My head continues to shake, denying reality. "I thought I could do this, but I can't. Please let me go. I'll find my way on my own." My panicked voice rises as hysteria sets in.

"You're not going anywhere."

I stare at him with disbelief and then a tinge of fear. "I don't want to stay here anymore." The anger returns to his eyes and I instantly regret my words. "I can't do this."

"Do what?" He nearly sneers the words. But his expression gives me the impression that he really wants to know.

"I just wanted to talk to you. I didn't mean for this." My voice trails off as I motion in the air between us.

"Do you only want Owen then?" I stare at him open-mouthed. The shame returns with a vengeance. I mumble my words to the floor as tears fall down my face. "This isn't what I came here for. I don't do this." I wipe my face and sniffle before looking into the beast's eyes, knowing I've fucked up badly. "I've never done this before. I didn't mean for it to happen. I'm sorry I offended you."

"I know."

"You know what?"

"That you haven't done this before. I can tell." His words crush the last bit of strength that I had. I thought he was enjoying it…I didn't realize I was so bad that he could tell I didn't know what I was doing. My voice catches as I try to respond, so I just slam my mouth shut. This wasn't a part of my plan. "Why are you so upset?"

"I'm sorry." I'm a blubbering fool. I'm so damn humiliated. "Please just leave me here."

"No."

He's not going to let me go. The realization hits me and tears prick at the back of my eyes. I regret my decision to follow them.

"Stop crying." I tilt my head back and stare at the ceiling through blurred vision, not knowing what to do or how to control myself. All I know is that I'm not okay. "I don't like it when you cry." I focus on my breathing and do my best to calm down. I need to figure a way out of this, and all of these emotions aren't helping.

I close my eyes and feel my chest heave. I concentrate on obeying the shifter. I don't want to make him any angrier than I already have. At this point I'm in unchartered waters, abandoned and lost and more emotional than I've ever felt in my life. This was such a bad idea.

Before I can scold myself anymore, Luke's strong arms wrap around my waist, lift me up, and pull me into his chiseled chest. My hands land on his hard pecs and I stare up at his gorgeous face through my lashes. The smothered fire in my core blazes to life.

CHAPTER FOUR

I can't fucking stand her crying. I've only been alone with her for less than an hour and I've already fucked this up. I knew this would happen. She's too different. There's no way she'll be able to handle both of us. She can't even handle me.

Or I can't handle her.

Jealousy seeps through me. If Owen were here, she wouldn't be crying. She was all over him. Rubbing her soft body against him, eager for his touch. She's terrified of me. What the hell does he have that I don't? We're twins for fuck's sake. Not that we look it. Or act like it. Whatever, he can have her. Even as I think the words, I know I'll never fucking stand for it.

She's mine.

My wolf snarls in my chest and I have to work damn hard to make sure my anger isn't showing. She's still cowering from me. What the fuck did I do that has her so fearful of me? She's my mate. Her body wants me, that much I'm certain of.

I'm not letting her run from me. I'm not going to lay back and watch her writhe under Owen's touch and avoid me. I can give her everything she needs and she's going to have to learn to take it and fucking deal with me and everything that comes with being my mate. She'll learn.

And she's going to start learning right fucking now.

I lift that sweet ass of hers up off the ground. My dick twitches at the sound of her shocked gasp. I fucking love that noise. Another wave of her arousal fills the cave and I know I'm not making this shit up. She may be scared of me, she may be second-guessing tracking us down, but she sure as hell wants me to fuck her. At least her body does. Her heat is going to hit her hard real fucking soon and I'll be sure to keep my dick in her as often as possible. Owen can wait in fucking line.

Her small hands land on my chest and her dark eyes look at me through thick lashes. I crush my lips on hers, pouring my frustration into the demanding kiss. Her breath mingles with mine and heats the air between us. I bite her bottom lip and squeeze her ass in my hands. She squeals and moans as my hands roam over her smooth skin, quickly ripping her clothes off. I'm aggressive with her small body, but I need to know she can handle this. I'll be as gentle as I can with her tight pussy, but this, me manhandling her, she needs to fucking get used to this. That little act she pulled earlier isn't going to fly with me. It's time she satisfied both of us. I know she wants me and now she's going to have to take me.

The deep need of desire rushes through my blood as she grips me back, kisses me back, moans with need into my mouth. I stare down at her and she's fucking gorgeous. My heart rages inside of me as the need to satisfy her takes over. She's going to love what I do to her. She'll want me more than him.

I drop to my knees on the ground with her still in my arms and flip her around, spreading her legs with my knees and rubbing my erection against her heat. I make no apologies for my straight forward-ness. I'm hard as steel and I can't fucking think with all the blood rushing to my dick. I need to unload and it's going to happen right fucking now. She could've done it with her mouth. I was easy on her. But even that little taste was too much for her.

I tried—even if it was just once—to go easy on her and to be gentle. She's the mate to a beast and she's going to take everything I give her. Owen may be gentle with her, but if it's up to me, Owen won't be having her to himself at all.

I look down at my beautiful mate, she's wait-ing patiently for my next command while breath-ing in heavy pants. I crave her like this. Wanting me. Desiring me. Submitting to me on all fours. Right now, I'm all she wants.

I stroke myself as my eyes travel over her curvy body. She's mine. All mine. I lean down and take a languid lick between her slit. Fucking delicious. My fingertips dig into her fleshy ass, holding her in place as I nip and suck her clit. She'll love how good of a mate I am to her. She'll love submitting to me.

I fucking love how she tries to pull away from the intense pleasure, but the moment my lips are off her she pushes her heat right back into my face. I breathe in her scent and smile before eating her out like I'm a starved man. Her pussy is my new favorite candy.

I pull away from her to look at her gorgeous curves. "Spread your cheeks for me." She looks back at me, a little lost for a moment, but then her face reddens with a beautiful blush that portrays her innocence. She lays her chest and head on the ground so she can reach behind her and put that pink pucker on display. Her pussy's glistening and I can't wait to feel all that warmth all over my dick.

"I—" She stutters into the ground as I push my hips against her with enough force that she realizes she's going to have to brace herself. I line up the head of my cock to her needy pussy and tease it a little, grinning to myself.

"I'm a virgin."

I hear her words at the same time that I slam all of my thick cock into her hot pussy. She screams into the ground as I still, buried to the hilt inside her. Her words and the feel of my dick buried inside her heat has my head thrown back in complete ecstasy. I fucking love that her first is all mine.

Fuck, she's so damn tight. I lean forward and put my chest on her back, staying deep inside her so she can adjust to my size, and kiss the tears on her cheeks.

I don't like that my little mate is in pain, but it'll be over soon, and then she'll be consumed with pleasure. There's an ache in my chest that grows with her obvious pain. I shush her and rock gently as I run my hands down her trembling body.

"Good girl." My hand reaches around to rub her tiny, throbbing clit. She feels too fucking good, and I know there's a possibility that I'll lose it the second her tight walls come around me. But I want this to be good for her. I *need* this to be good for her. She needs to love this. I strum her clit and kiss all over her slender neck, soothing her trembling body. She's so small under me. So fragile.

I need to contain this beast in me. I need to hold back. She's only human and I have to remember that. She can't take me like I want her to. The thought makes me angry, and I don't realize how aggressive I'm being on her clit until she's spasming under me. She cries out into the ground as her body tenses and her walls pulse around my dick. Shit. I'm going to fucking come just from that. I breathe in her scent and focus on the fact that I'm her first. This right here, she's going to remember this forever. I nip her neck and I rock into her again and again, upping her pleasure and pushing her higher and higher. Her pants are ragged as her body relaxes under me and those mewls of pleasure come easier and easier.

I take a few deep breaths, put one hand on the small of her back and grip her hip with the other. "Hold still." *Go easy on her.* I pump in and out thinking the words each time. *Go easy on her.* I'm trying my fucking best, I really am. But fuck! All I want to do is rut her beautiful ass into the ground. Her scent, her feel, this pull… *she's mine.*

Her breasts bounce and her ass joggles with my movements and I find myself picking up the pace, mesmerized by her gorgeous curves.

"Harder," she mewls. My fist tightens on her hip. *Did I hear her right?* I slam into her tight heat, loving the way she pushes back, and I practically howl in triumph. I pump faster. She's moaning into the ground and pushing back just as much. *Fuck yes.*

"Take it." I growl into her ear as I pound ruthlessly into her. Her body jolts and convulses as I take another orgasm from her. I circle her clit, drawing out her pleasure as she screams my name.

That's right. *MY* name.

Her virgin pussy is mine. All fucking mine.

I'm close to my release, but I want her to come with me. I pull out of her and flip her onto her back.

I want a better view of her face when I come inside her for the first time. She gasps as her back hits the ground and for a second I think I've hurt her, but she tilts her hips up; her pussy begs to be filled again. I smirk down at her and thrust all the way in. She throws her head back and screams her pleasure in the air between us. One hand flies to her throat and the other strums her glistening clit. She's so fucking wet, her honey drips out of her and down to her ass. I squeeze her throat and pound into her tight pussy. "Eyes on me, sugar." Her eyes pop open and I keep her gaze. "Don't fucking close your eyes."

Her breasts bounce with each hard thrust and her whimpering moans fill the cave. The sound of me rutting into her combined with her little noises is a symphony to my ears. I want this. I want this with her every single day for the rest of my life. The tingle in my spine grows larger and my toes go numb. I'm going to unload in her sweet pussy any second now. I circle her clit with more pressure and stare deep into her dark eyes as I take her to the edge with me. Right on cue, she comes for me, and she keeps her eyes on me the entire time. Her lips part and let out a strangled cry as her body tenses. *So fucking beautiful.*

I keep up the shallow pumps, milking out every

bit of my orgasm with her body. Her whimpers of pleasure with each small thrust makes me leak even more into her. Our combined come leaks out of her heat and down her thighs. I fucking love that I'm already marking her.

Just as I lean down to give her soft lips a kiss, intending on giving her every bit of affection I can, Owen storms in the cave and stares at me as though I'm his enemy. Knowing we're both her mates, that she could choose one of us and leave the other, I agree with the sentiment. I've never wished ill upon my brother, my twin, but as his silver eyes heat with rage and his fists clench, in this moment, I know I'd kill him for my mate.

CHAPTER FIVE

Emma

"**W**HAT THE FUCK ARE YOU DOING?" Owen's voice booms through the cave and clears the lust clouding my head. His words are dripping with hatred. Fear engulfs me although I'm still trembling from what Luke made me feel. I swallow thickly and try to sit up and move away from Luke. A low growl tears from his throat as his blunt nails dig into the flesh of my hips, holding me under him. His eyes narrow, warning me. The pull I felt to him just a moment ago wanes. The haze clears and confusion clouds my judgment. The man I gave myself to has changed before my eyes and I instantly regret what I've done.

I felt alive for the first time. I felt a spark of electricity each time he moved inside of me. It felt…perfect. There's no other word to describe it. Him taking me like that felt like it was meant to happen this way. What a foolish thought. I've never been so stupid in my entire life. I've abandoned all sense of judgment.

How could I've let that happened? My breath hitches as Owen's angered steps shake the floor. He's pissed. Luke has yet to break eye contact with me since I've tried to move away from him. I'm frozen in place. Stuck between the rage of the two shifters. Hot blood rushes in my ears as my body goes numb with fear.

"Get off her, you selfish prick." Owen snarls his words. "She's not just for you. How fucking dare you take her without me!" His words bellow in the cave and ring loud in my ears. They fucking hurt. I don't know what I thought, or why I have such strong feelings for them, but to know it's not reciprocated. My throat dries, choking me. I finally break away and stare at the wall of the cave—away from Luke, away from Owen. I can't stand the emotions overwhelming me.

"What? You're fine with her being a human, just not my leftovers?" My heart crumples and falls in my chest. Is that what I am now? I bared myself to him and now I'm "leftovers"? I'm a used-up fuck toy for them to share?

What a fucking prick. I grab my clothes off the floor and pull them to my chest, covering myself. I can't look at either of them. I thought werewolves were monogamous. I thought they saved themselves for their mate. It's the impression I got from all of the offerings I've attended. I've studied every video, every little nuisance. How did I get that so wrong?

What the fuck did I just do?

"How could you fucking do that to me, Luke?" Owen's harsh words make my body crumple with guilt. My breath comes in rushed pants as I push away all the emotions threatening to consume me. This isn't anything that I prepared for. I've spent years pining for a chance to meet a werewolf and discover the secrets of their supernatural world. And this is what I've done with it. I've become a prisoner and allowed myself to submit to their desires for my body. I need to get the hell out of here. My entire body is numb with regret.

"Fuck you." Luke's response isn't screamed or

snarled. It's a simple statement from a low voice devoid of emotion. And somehow, that makes him even more terrifying. I glance between the two shifters, and I have no idea which is the Alpha. I don't understand their hierarchy. I expect to see anger from Owen, but instead there's only hurt in his eyes. Luke finally moves away from me, and I close my legs and turn my body away from them. Shame heats my cheeks once again.

As he leaves the cave, Luke intentionally bumps his right half hard against Owen's shoulder and chest. Then all hell breaks loose. Owen's hard fist lands with a loud smash to Luke's jaw. The two shifters' fists are clenched so tight that their muscles must be screaming in pain as they land blow after blow, punching each other in the side, the chest, anywhere they can. They collide into each other and smash their bodies against the rock before tumbling to the ground. I can't help the screams ripping from my throat. I struggle in the dirt to push my body against the wall and keep myself far away from them.

Blood drips from their wounded knuckles as bruises appear and fade before my eyes. The cave vibrates with fury as they snarl and growl, rolling over one another and locking each other's arms to avoid further damage. For a moment it looks as though it's a stalemate, but then Owen's head smashes into Luke's nose. Blood streams down his face.

"Stop it!" I scream at them as hot tears burn down my cheeks. My throat blisters as I scream over and over, pleading for them to stop. The sight of them beating each other so savagely has my heart beating chaotically with fear. Neither holds back.

As their massive forms move to the back of the cave, each in a body lock by the other, I catch sight of the opening, the light floods my vision, and I bolt. I push my legs to run faster than I ever have before. I'm not a fool, they'll catch me if they want to. I can't outrun a shifter, I can't hide from their heightened senses, but I can get a head start. Maybe they'll let me go. I'm not worth the trouble.

As the thought hits me, I stumble on the ground, scraping my knees as my legs give out beneath me and my forearms land hard on the unforgiving ground. I cry out with a nearly unbearable pain. I've given my virginity to a stranger and now I'm running from him, from them, and hoping that I'm not worth the energy. I allow myself only a moment of regret and sadness before picking my body up and continuing my escape. My knees sting as the scrapes are pulled with each movement, but I keep pushing myself, fueling my motivation with the memory of them hurtling their large fists at each other with the intent to do extreme damage.

This was such a mistake. How was I so wrong about them? I haphazardly brush the tears away as I tear through branches on my careless descent down a large hill. My ankle nearly twists as I slip on one rock and then another, but I keep my balance and push my limbs harder, accepting the burn as my punishment.

I hope I never see them again. Either of them. My heart twists with wretched pain and I gasp for air as another painful sob racks through my body. It's a lie. A very large part of me wants them to chase me. But I don't want to be a chew toy they fight over. I'm worth more than a simple fuck, and I'll be no one's leftovers. I cling to the words that each of them used to hurt me, hoping that one day I'll really believe that I don't want to see them. My mind is at war with itself, with regret and with want. It's a torture I've never felt.

Fuck, they both hardly said a word to me. Tears fall harder at the realization. All Luke said to me was "suck" before I bent over and let him take a part of me that I'll never have again. It was hot as fuck to hear that word from his lips and made me crave his touch more than I've ever wanted anything, but that's all he said to me. My body tingles with fatigue and sharp pains shoot through my legs all the way to my lungs. I don't know how far I've run, but it's most likely laughably short compared to the ability of the shifters.

I slow as I near a stream. My face is hot and my lungs hurt with each heavy breath. I wipe my remaining tears before collapsing by the water and splashing my face. The cool water calms my hot skin, but also makes me want to throw up. Or maybe it's just the situation that has me feeling so sick. I gently rock my body as I try to calm my breathing. I turn, looking for my backpack and clothes, only to realize I've left both. I'm naked and alone. I have no idea where I am or how long it'll be until I find civilization. I can't believe what's happened. It's unreal.

My body shudders with fear and regret. For the first time in a long time, I feel completely and utterly alone and helpless. *What the fuck have I done?*

CHAPTER SIX

Owen

I T ONLY TOOK A MOMENT. A VERY SHORT moment, to notice she was gone. Her absence rocked the very core of me. A coldness set deep in my limbs. So numbing I let go of my hold on Luke and didn't even flinch as his fist hit my cheek bone, cracking something, although I'm not sure what. Blood fills my mouth, but all I can concentrate on is the opening to the cave. My chest aches and my wolf whines. *She's hurt.*

"You hurt her!" I scream at Luke and shove him into the back of the cave.

"You hurt her! Not me!" he screams in my face,

so close that his spit hits my chin. His shoulders rock with fury and he glares at me with spite. "She fucking loved what I did to her." He snarls his words and beats his fist against his chest. "I felt her affection, the spark between us." He sneers at me and starts walking toward the light filtering in the cave. "You ruined it. You ruined this."

I yank his shoulder and force him to look at me. He's not going to blame this all on me. "You took her. I smell her blood!" His eyes leave mine and flash with guilt. "How could you do that to me?" A pain of betrayal hurts my chest. Never once have we fought against each other like this. When our older brother left, forfeiting the pack, our father, our Alpha... We never would've survived without each other. We have always had each other's back. Through all of the bullshit. Yet here we are, finally with a pack of our own, thriving, and we come to blows over our shared mate. "You think I want to share her? I don't!" His eyes meet mine again with a challenge. "But I'd never do that to you!"

"Bullshit!" His words are full of anger, but also full of doubt.

"I wouldn't hurt you like that. You know what it would mean to have our mate deny either one of us." Even the thought of her choosing just one of us nearly crumples my body. There's no way we could remain Alphas. Not with the pain and weakness it would cause our wolves. Death would be better. At least that would be honorable.

"My intent wasn't to hurt you." He glances at the entrance and then meets my gaze before clenching his fists. "It wasn't about you. I wasn't thinking like that."

"You weren't thinking at all!" I yell at him. Although he doesn't flinch or react in the least, I see his eyes flash with remorse.

It takes several minutes for us to calm the fuck down; I feel my muscles relax and my skin heal as I stretch my arms and rub my jaw. "Well maybe with your dick." I try to lighten the mood between us. After all, Luke has never been a peacemaker, and I want this behind us as soon as possible. We need to be united for the sake of our mate. He huffs at my remark, devoid of all humor. I crack my neck and give him a look over. "At least I got to beat your ass." I lean my neck to one side until it cracks and then the other side. "I've always wondered who would win between the two of us."

"Bullshit, you got your ass handed to you." A semblance of a smile barely surfaces, but the air between us feels cleaner. I smack a hand on his solid back and start walking out of the cave.

My smile slips and I glance into the woods, sniffing the air for her scent. "We need to find her and make it up to her." She couldn't have gotten very far, but she's hurt. I can feel it in my bones. Darkness washes over Luke as he nods his head. My chest pains looking at him. If only I'd kept my emotions in check, she wouldn't be hurting. This could've been so good. Fuck, if I hadn't been pissed, we could both be satisfying our sweet mate right now. I shake my head and look at the ground while taking a deep breath. "We'll make it up to her."

"We have to." Luke's solemn words ring in my ears and we head into the woods.

It's easy to catch her scent. It's the sweetest thing in the air. It's also mixed with my brother's scent, and I have to restrain myself from getting pissed all over again. I forgive him, but I'm going to fucking remember this. We should've taken her together. Her virginity was just as much mine as it was his. A low growl rumbles in my chest as the thought registers. Luke looks my way and has the decency to at least look a little shameful.

"I want her next…alone." Luke's jaw clenches and

he looks like he wants to fight me. My eyes widen in surprise. He's got to be fucking kidding me! I clench my fist, hoping I don't have to lay into him, but I'm fucking ready if he's going to be stubborn.

"Fine." He barely grumbles the word through clenched teeth.

"And her ass." I add that in there more or less to let him know her ass is mine. His eyes blaze with fury.

"Fuck off." He spits his words and starts running, shifting in the air and landing hard on the ground, before taking off toward our mate. Selfishly I correct myself, *my mate.*

CHAPTER SEVEN

Emma

I SHIVER ON THE GROUND, NOT WANTING TO move, but knowing I need to get going. My body is aching with a soreness I've never experienced in my life. I clench my thighs and my pussy aches. I wince and moan into the ground. It's not a good ache. Not at all. Tears prick and they're purely from the pain. And then I remember. I remember Luke and his authority, his desire for my body. I remember his eyes as he watched me find my release. The feeling of him inside of me.

My heart clenches in my chest with desperation and a sadness I've never imagined I could feel. I hear his word "leftovers." I cry harder into the ground. I've never been hurt so much in my life. I'm saddened by Owen and what he really thinks of me. I don't know how I managed to feel so much for men I don't even know. I can't believe I've given so much of myself to each of them. Physically and emotionally.

I wince and remember them fighting. Fighting over me. Over their plaything. I fist my hands and pound them into the dirt in frustration, but also the need to feel something other than this sadness. Each movement reminds me of the soreness between my thighs.

I pick my body up off the ground slowly, relishing the pain. I fucking deserve this. What did I honestly expect, coming here, hunting down wolves? What a fucking idiot I was.

I've sacrificed my whole life in order to research their species. I have no friends. I've lost all contact over the years as I've traveled from town to town, questioning as many people as I could about the shift-ers. I've interviewed dozens, if not more, of families of the women who were taken. None of them had ever heard from their loved ones after they'd been taken. They also never understood why they were so at peace and calm while they were being taken from their homes.

That was my first clue. Werewolves don't possess magic. They can't calm someone with a touch like a witch can. Yet each time, the women go easily, willingly with the wolves. The only exception was the Shadow Falls' offering. I still don't understand what happened, and I intend to get to the bottom of it. I watched the news clip of the women. Elizabeth and Grace. I saw how the shifters calmed the women. How they looked at them. With devotion and love. There's no doubt in my mind that there was true love between them. I studied the historical texts over and over, searching for a hint of human and werewolf relations.

I didn't find anything. Nothing at all. But I found old scripts about beasts and their fated mates. Tales of how the beast was only tamed by his beauty. True love. I believed in a legend. A fairytale. I was a fucking idiot. Fairytales are for children. Romantic knights in shining armor are for books; there aren't princes waiting to come rescue damsels in distress. I look down at my battered, aching body and feel as irrational as I look.

I wrap my arms around my chest and look into

the woods. I haven't a clue which way is safe or where I'll end up. I know we were heading toward Shadow Falls, toward the Dark Valley. So I'm not fucking going in that direction. Fuck that.

I start to walk in the opposite direction, the way we came, but stop immediately. That would mean more than a full day in the woods. So I turn ninety degrees and start walking. I can't remember on the map what it is that I'm walking toward, but at least I'm walking away from the asshole shifters.

I sigh and push my hand against my chest to relieve some of the pain. It fucking hurts to be leaving them behind me. It physically pains me. My body shudders with the cold, but also with a sense of loneliness.

What is wrong with me? My head hasn't been right since I first saw them.

I was dead wrong.

Werewolves don't have fated mates; they don't hold the offerings so they can claim the ones they love. A deep frown mars my face as unwanted emotions settle in. Not paying attention, I step on a pine cone or nut or something that really fucking hurts. As I shriek and pull back, my bare back falls against a tree and I suck air through my clenched teeth to keep from screaming as I grab my foot. Fuck! My eyes stay closed shut and I start rubbing the sore spot with my thumbs. The pain slowly subsides and just as I'm about to put my foot down and continue my probably-going-to-lead-to-death journey, a large, warm hand takes my foot. My eyes pop open and I scream in terror. My hand shoots to my chest as the air freezes in my lungs and I stare at Owen's massive chest. He's kneeling, but his chest is at my eye level.

My heart pounds. *He came for me.*

I resist the urge to lean into him. The force between us threatens to make me submit to him once again. I have to remind myself what happened. And what he thinks of me. I can't let myself fall for him. I can't be blinded by lust like I was by Luke.

But his fingers massaging my aching foot feel so damn good. The heady haze comes over me once again. His kind silver eyes don't meet mine. He concentrates on the small red mark on the arch of my foot. My eyes travel up his muscular arm to his broad shoulders and down his chiseled chest. His tanned skin tempts my fingertips to run along rippled muscle. I feel a strange urge to lick his neck. To nip his ear lobe.

Every thought I had only moments ago drifts

away. I can't think of anything other than his touch and how easily he could make me feel better.

I want nothing more than for him to make this pain go away. Innately, I know he can. I know he *wants* to.

My eyes roam his body, causing my pussy to clench and dampen. Owen's head falls back and his lips part with the sexiest groan I've ever heard. The sight of his throat. Holy fuck, it makes my libido scorch for him. A werewolf exposed his throat to me. I still don't know if he's an Alpha. Especially after what happened in the cave. But Alpha or not, exposing a throat is nearly identical to bowing. Another wave of lust rolls through me and has my toes curling as I resist my instincts.

His silver eyes heat as he sets my foot down and takes a step away from me.

"First, I'm making one thing absolutely clear." His voice is so fucking sexy I hardly hear his words. He inhales a deep breath, closing his eyes and shuddering with desire. "Then I'll take care of you." The way his eyes stare into mine with primal need causes a wave of fear to hit me. But it's gone as quickly as it came.

"We're not letting you leave." His words are hard and final, but his eyes linger on my throat and he licks his lips. The action distracts me and it takes a moment for the words to register.

Suddenly I'm aware of everything that happened. Of what they said. It's like a bullet to my heart and a goddamn ice bath between my legs.

What the fuck? I haven't had enough punishment already?

"Fuck you!" The words fly out of my mouth before I'm able to stop them. Anger makes his eyes narrow and nostrils flare. My small hands fly to my mouth in horror. What the hell is wrong with me? I must truly have a death wish. I shrink as he takes a step toward me.

"Don't worry, sweetness, you will be fucking me. There's no doubt about that."

"You know what? I'm going to die out here anyway. I guess it doesn't really matter how." Tears leak from my eyes as I scream at his face, his chest really. "Fuck you! I'm not some damn toy for you and Luke to pass around. I deserve better than that. I deserve better than either of you!" Shock and then remorse passes across his face.

"Toy?" He seems genuinely hurt and confused. Like they weren't talking about me like I was a plaything that they didn't want to share.

"You said so yourself. That I wasn't just for Luke." I spit the words with distaste and try to keep my shoulders squared and my words hard, but my voice and my composure crack. I stifle my emotions and continue to glare at him.

"You *aren't* just for him." I turn my back to him and brush my shoulder against the tree as I walk away. Fuck him. I hope he breaks my neck for disrespecting him. I really do. I don't want this ache of regret in my chest. I just want it all to end.

His strong arms wrap around my body and pull me into his hard chest. I try pushing away, but I'm so fucking weak. It doesn't take long for me to give up. I just don't have any strength left. I hang my head in shame and wait for him to do what he will.

He loosens his grip and turns me into his chest, letting me bury my head in his chest as he rubs my back. I don't know why he's attempting to calm me, but I'll fucking take it. I need a peaceful touch. The day has taken too much out of me.

I dare to pull away from him to look up at his face. He's so damn sad. He looks wretched with re-morse. He leans down to kiss me, slowly. Slow enough for me to turn my head away. I want to kiss him. My soul is begging me to kiss him. But I refuse. I'm not going to fall for it again. Not after what happened with Luke. I'm not going to be anyone else's *leftovers*.

A low, warning growl rumbles in his chest and vibrates through my entire body. I close my eyes in fear, but I hold my ground.

"Kiss me." It's a command and I feel a crushing weight on my body to obey. But I close my eyes tighter and prepare for his rage. My breath fails me and I feel lightheaded. But I'm not going to fucking do it.

"Kiss me." I can feel his eyes on me as he speaks his words louder. As though I didn't hear him the first time. I feel the weight of his dominance and nearly crumble. I shake my head and whimper as his grip on me tightens.

I'm ready for death. A sob rips through me and I almost cave and turn into him to kiss his soft lips. Lips that I desperately want to feel against mine. But I can't. I won't let myself be demeaned. Not again.

His grip only tightens more. "Why?" Pain laces his words. I don't expect it. My eyelids part and I peek at him through my lashes. He looks nothing but hurt. "What have I done that's so horrible that you won't kiss me? You're willing to mate with my brother, but you won't even kiss me?"

His brother? Luke and Owen are brothers? He must see my confusion.

"Twins." I shake my head slightly. I'm not sure why, maybe to clear the haze coming over me. "Do you only feel the pull to him?" His eyes portray fear and he noticeably swallows, waiting for my reply. His fingers dig into me, not to hurt, but just to hold onto me. As though he's holding onto hope.

A thick lump grows in my throat. I barely squeak out the word "pull." He nods his head once, not willing to explain anymore and still demanding an answer. A pull? I have strong unexplained feelings for both of them. I don't understand it. A pull? I suppose I would call it that. Owen shifts slightly on his feet but maintains eye contact.

I have to lower my head and stare at his chest to tell him the truth. "I feel something for both of you." A heavy sigh of relief leaves him as he pulls me into his chest, lifting my feet off the ground and kissing my hair. I sigh softly and nuzzle into his chest, enjoying the affection. But then I remember, I can't forget. And I push away, not wanting to be swayed into making the same mistake. What is wrong with me? What is the pull?

He looks down at me with the same hurt in his

eyes, but his brows are furrowed in confusion. "Why do you keep denying me? What have I done?"

I can't speak, but I'm sure my expression says enough. Disbelief and outrage are all I can feel, and I hope he can see that.

His eyes widen and he leans back to give me room. "What did I do?"

"Well for starters the only word you've said to me is 'come.' And then you burst in while I was…while…" I flail my arms and shove his hands off me. I need space; I can barely breathe let alone speak. "And you talk about sharing me. And then you fight over me, like I'm some sort of prize."

"You don't understand." I part my lips to lay into him yet again, apparently I've completely lost my mind and my filter. Stupid. I'm still being stupid. He gently places a large finger across my lips and gives me a pleading look to listen to him. When I narrow my eyes the look turns into a warning. I pull away from him and stare at the dirt before deciding to hear him out. He waits to speak until I look at him.

His hand cups my chin and his thumb rubs along my bottom lip. I almost pull away, but it's so comforting I can't. "I can't speak to you in wolf form. I'm very sorry I didn't take a moment to talk to you when I could. We needed to travel quickly, and I wanted to keep you warm at night, that's why I stayed wolf. As for fighting over you…" He looks into the trees behind me, back the way we came, before staring into my eyes again. I nearly turn to see if Luke is behind me, but his hand keeps me facing him.

"I'm not ashamed to say I fought for you." His piercing eyes reflect his honesty. "And I'd do it again if I had to." I shake my head and try to free myself from his hold. He doesn't let me go though. "I won't deny it and I won't lie to you. I am sorry I hurt you though. That wasn't my intention." His sweet words tempt me to melt into him, but I hold on to the last bit of dignity I have.

"I'm not a fuck toy. I refuse to be demeaned like that."

Owen's hard words make me flinch. "You are not a fuck toy! You will not talk about yourself like that ever again. Do you hear me?" My shoulders collapse and fear cripples me. I whimper and nod my head as my shoulders hunch in.

"And you are not leaving. You. Are. Our. Mate." He growls the words and at first, fear is all I register. But as the words sink in, I feel my shoulders open and my fear lifts. A warmth settles in my chest as I look into Owen's silver gaze. The anger on his face dissipates as he sees my expression.

"Mate?"

He nods his head as his forehead pinches. "Yes." His hand gently pushes my hair behind my ear, and he strokes my cheek with his thumb. "You're our mate. Do you know what that means?"

A small smile graces my lips as I shake my head. I have an idea and if it's anything like I've fantasized… I need to hear him say it. My heart flutters in my chest with need, but my breathing stills, waiting to hear the words.

"It means you're ours forever, you are the one fate chose for us." A weight lifts off my body and I breathe in an easy breath. A blush heats my cheeks as my smile widens without my consent.

"You like that, don't you?"

Is this real? I nod and whisper my response. "I do."

All I keep thinking is that this cannot be real.

I brush my hand along his dark stubble and love the prickly feel. I was right. Werewolves have mates. And I'm his. My eyes widen as I realize he said *our*. "Both of yours?" I blink several times waiting for him to respond.

"Yes." His word is clipped, and I can tell he's

holding something back. "So long as you'll have us, we're both yours." The way he says it makes me heat with desire. His nostrils flare and he licks his lips.

He groans out, "You need me, sweetness." The sheer heat in his gaze makes my thighs clench with a need I've never known before. I nod, not trusting my voice, and the second I do, his lips are on mine. That lust-filled haze comes again and I mindlessly wonder if that's what he meant by pull. This all-consuming desire.

His tongue slips past my lips and explores my mouth. He suckles my upper lip, teasing it and making me moan. His hands find my waist and lifts me into his chest as he lays me down on the ground. I moan into his mouth. Wanting more, *needing* more. My legs part for him and there's not an ounce of shame—only want. I feel his fingers on my clit and gasp at the sheer intensity of the pleasure it gives me. My back bows off the ground as he slips his finger into me, curling it and hitting my g-spot. I whimper as his finger leaves me, but he only adds a second and goes right back to finger fucking me and making my body heat and numb with my impending orgasm.

Yes! Fuck, yes. I moan loudly into the air, but he takes my mouth with his, smothering the noise. He shifts on top of me with one hand planted on the ground by my head, allowing his body to cage me in. The other leaves my heat, but before I think of protesting, he's lining the head of his cock at my opening. My body tenses, on edge and waiting for release.

He doesn't thrust into me like Luke did. He's not aggressive at all. Instead he moves slowly, his girth stretching my walls. I writhe under him as he stills deep inside me. The slight pain only adds to the intense pleasure. My body craves more while also demanding I move away. My head shakes on the ground as he moves slowly in and out of my aching warmth. Each thrust is slow and careful. Bringing me to the edge, but not taking me over. I bite my lip and stare at his face, the epitome of rapture. His eyes are closed and his lips part as he continues his slow assault. Pulling nearly all the way out and then burying himself to the hilt.

"More," I beg, pushing my hips to meet his. My clit throbs for attention and my nails dig in the dirt, trying to just hold on. "Please." I don't give a fuck that I'm begging. My breath comes in heavy pants. "Faster."

Owen's eyes glow as he looks down at me and shakes his head. "No." I part my lips to protest just as he pushes into me again, and instead of words, a strangled moan vibrates past my lips. So close, but so far away. My head thrashes on the ground as he continues his pace, pushing the limit of my pleasure to an intensity I've never experienced. My back arches and my hand instinctively flies to my clit. Needing that pressure to bring me over. Just a small touch would do.

His hand grabs my wrist and pins it above my head. "Don't you fucking dare." He growls his words, and the sound of his rugged voice only heightens my pleasure. I scream and beg for him to give me what I need. "You will get what I give you, when I give it to you." Fuck, his words send another wave of arousal to soak where we meet. He groans and clenches his teeth but doesn't increase his pace.

Both of them, both my mates, are aggressive and hard, but each in their own way. Luke gave me every pleasure without reservation, Owen is holding back. I need more. I crave more. His hand slides down my body as he kisses me with passion and raw heat.

I murmur a plea into his mouth as he kisses me. His lips leave mine, and I part my eyes to find him watching me intently. "You ready to come for me, sweetness?"

Without warning he slams into me and circles

his thumb on my clit. His motions are nearly violent as my body bucks beneath him. A blinding light flashes before my eyes as he pounds into me mercilessly. My body tenses and trembles, frozen yet heated with the stunning pleasure. My lips open but nothing comes out. My pussy clamps down on his dick and my release tears through me viciously. My body shakes. As I stare blindly ahead, I make out Luke in the trees. I'm paralyzed with pleasure and unable to truly recognize what's happening. And then I realize I've been screaming. A cold wave washes through me as my body numbs and spasms. Although I'm staring at Luke, I cry out Owen's name.

CHAPTER EIGHT

After a moment of steady breathing my body calms; Owen's hands are roaming over my body as are his lips. The light touches make my body shudder and spasm with aftershocks. I push against his shoulders in an attempt to make him stop. It's too much.

I can feel his smile as he chuckles into my stomach. "Greedy girl, aren't you?" I look down my body at him and watch as he kisses his way farther down my stomach.

"No, no!" I shake my head as I realize his intent.

"I didn't mean that. I can't." His low, rough chuckle tickles my belly.

"You could." He teases me and licks his lips. The sight sends a wave of desire through me and as I instinctively clench, I wince from the slight pain. I'm so sore. He sees my reaction and climbs up my body, kissing the tender spot in the crook of my neck. A shiver of pleasure runs through my body as he rolls me into him. I cuddle into his chest, rubbing my cheek against his hard chest. I close my eyes, savoring this moment. This is what I thought it would be like when I lost my virginity. My eyes open remembering Luke. I twist in Owen's arms and look through the trees, searching for him.

"What are you looking for?" Owen massages the curve in my waist and kisses my neck again.

I feel guilty thinking of Luke while I'm in Owen's arms. My arms cross over my breasts and I turn away from him, hating myself for ruining the moment. Owen gently places an arm around me and molds his chest to my back. "Are you cold?"

At his question I realize that I am a bit chilly, so I nod and bite the inside of my cheek. "I was looking for Luke." I blush and stare at the ground. "I thought I saw him."

Owen doesn't seem bothered in the least by my confession. "He was here earlier; I'm not sure if he stayed." He kisses me one last time before rising to his feet and towering over me. He holds a hand down to me and I give him a small grateful simper and take it. I'm grateful for many things, but mostly that he's not hurt that I was looking for Luke.

I wish I'd had this with him. Would he have held me close and kissed me so sweetly like Owen did? I press my lips into a tight line. I doubt it. I highly doubt it. My face heats with mortification and my eyes widen as I remember screaming Owen's name while locking eyes with Luke. My heart hardens and tries to leap through my throat. I can't believe I did that. My breath quickens and I frantically look through the trees again. He must feel so hurt. I feel like an absolute bitch. It wasn't done intentionally; he must know that.

"What's wrong, sweetness?" I can't help the small smile that comes to my lips at his pet name for me.

"Sweetness?" I question him and try to ease the worry in my chest. I'll just apologize to Luke. I'm sure things will be all right. Especially now that I know we're mates. I can't wait to write about this. It's going to open everyone's eyes and aid the cause to combine our worlds.

"Yeah." He playfully nips my neck. "You smell sweet and you taste sweet." He wraps a large arm around my waist and picks me up, making me squeal. He kisses my shoulder and gives my ass a slap. "And now I've got to get your sweet ass home."

Home. To a pack. As their mate.

So much has happened so quickly and my head swarms with questions. He gently sets me down on the ground and takes my hand in his to lead me back the way we came.

"Where is home?" I'm all too aware I haven't agreed to anything, and I'm not sure if I said no what would happen. I'm also not sure what they'll say when I tell them my intent.

"The Dark Valley." I stop in my tracks.

"By Shadow Falls?"

He looks down at me with confusion. "Yes."

"But what about the other pack?"

"Devin's pack?" I nod my head, all too aware of the details of that pack that were released. I'll never forget the looks on the women's faces at the Shadow Falls offering.

"How could two packs be so close together? And why would you want to be close to that pack?"

"You talk like you know of his pack."

"I saw the offering. There's no way they were mates." I bite my bottom lip, realizing I've given him more information than I intended.

"Sweet and smart." He grins down at me cockily. "They are their mates."

I shake my head. "No, they weren't. Did you see what happened?" There's no way with the way they reacted.

"I did. It's complicated, but my brother assured me that they are mates to his pack members." I furrow my brows.

"How would Luke know?" He shakes his head as we continue to walk back to the cave.

"Not Luke, Jude. Our older brother. He's a member of Devin's pack."

"Why isn't he a part of your pack?"

"Long story." I almost protest, but he comes to the conclusion I was going to argue. Before I can speak, he says, "I guess we have time." He sighs heavily and lifts a branch higher so I don't have to duck below it.

"Our father was an…unjust Alpha. He didn't approve of any kind of weakness or challenge to authority. Jude is the oldest and then there's Luke and me." I nod my head, keeping up with his tale as I hold his hand to keep my balance climbing up the hill. I hardly have any energy left. Owen takes pity on me and reaches down to pick me up. He holds me to his chest and walks as though I weigh nothing in his arms. His warmth and scent are everything.

Again I'm reminded of the pull, and without a doubt, I can feel it. It steals away my logic and everything other than *him*. My mate.

"So it was just you three?" Owen nods his head, and a sadness crosses his face. "Our mother passed giving birth to us. So we were raised by our father, the Alpha." He clears his throat and continues to walk at a leisurely pace. "When we were in our young teens, a seer told our father that his son would challenge him. And that he would win, killing our father in the process." I part my lips in shock.

"A seer?" What is a seer?

"Someone who can see glimpses of the future." Well I suppose I could've figured that out on my own. "They're never wrong."

"So one of you three killed your father?"

Owen shakes his head. "No, he still lives. He was convinced we would though." He breathes deep. "We had to leave shortly after the seer gave him the news. He became an entirely different person. He was unstable and abusive. Jude took the brunt of it. Jude told us to leave one night. He'd overheard our father talking to the Betas." His eyes focus ahead. "They were trying to convince him not to kill us."

A chill runs through me as I stare up at him. He doesn't look down at me though. How fucking awful that a father would consider murdering his own children. I vaguely wonder if it's common, but I don't ask. I don't interrupt. "So we left that night and about a week later, we heard that Jude had left and we weren't sure where he'd gone. We met some interesting creatures along the way and decided to make our own pack. We were nomads for a while until Jude got a hold of us and Devin offered us the land next to theirs."

"But what about hunting grounds?" Owen's rough laugh bellows in the air.

"We rarely hunt." He kisses my cheek and moves a hand to my ass to squeeze. "Times have changed. Some packs still hunt and have temporary camps, but most are stable and have means of revenue."

"Oh, I didn't know that. What does your pack do?" I wish I had my notebook so I could write this all down. I don't want to forget anything.

"We have a tech company. We were just over at the University. We've got a good co-op going on over there and we needed an update. But it's sensitive information."

"Are you serious?" He's gotta be shitting me.

He laughs at my disbelief. "Yes."

"So werewolves are tech geeks?"

"Well no, just your mates and the Alphas of Dark Valley."

"There are two Alphas?"

"Yup. Your mates."

I still in his arms. "You're the Alpha? You're both Alphas?"

"What about me?" Luke's question comes out hard and angry. That aggression shoots a need to my clit. His low, menacing voice reminds me of what happened between us.

"You're her Alpha and her mate." Owen's response is clipped but doesn't hold any aggression toward him. I feel awkward in his arms with Luke's eyes on me.

"I am." His blue eyes roam my body before falling to the ground as he turns his back toward us. "We need to go, it's getting late."

"Could I talk to you for a second?" I don't know how I manage to get the words out.

"You want some privacy?" I nod my head once at Owen's question and squeeze his hand in thanks.

Luke turns back to face me as Owen sets me down and heads toward the cave. It's in sight and not even a quarter mile away. Time passes and tensions grow between us with the silence. I can barely look him in the eyes. I twist my fingers in my hand and try to figure out what words I want to say. Luke waits patiently, although his eyes are focused intently on me, and his intense glare makes me uncomfortable. He looks pissed. Or emotionless. It's hard to tell which.

"I didn't mean to hurt you." I hesitantly start. "With what happened back there."

"You didn't." His tone lacks all emotion, and his face keeps that dark, intense expression. I shift uncomfortably.

"I just thought you may have been feeling a

certain way." I drift as my eyes look everywhere but back at that damn stare of his. I want to feel better, since he's saying he wasn't hurt. But the way he's acting makes me feel differently.

"I'm not. So don't worry about me. I don't care if you fuck him. He can have you." His words cut me to the core. Fuck, that hurt.

"You don't want me?" The very thought makes a sickening knot twist in my gut. He was my first. Owen told me he was my mate. Does that mean nothing to him?

He huffs a humorless laugh. "Doesn't matter if I want you or not." He walks closer to me and stands just inches away from me. Crowding my space and forcing me to crane my neck to keep eye contact. "Once your heat hits, you'll be begging me to fuck you. It's going to be fun claiming your ass while you're in heat." His snide remark pisses me off. What an asshole. I came to apologize and he's going to talk to me like that? Well, fuck him.

I walk around him, feeling colder by the second, and head toward the cave, not looking back to say a damn word to him. I've given him enough. There's no fucking way I'll ever let him touch me again. I don't know what the hell a heat is or claiming for that matter. But it's not going to happen. I'll follow them to their pack, but only to get my story. I'm not sticking around to deal with this. It sucks that I'll have to leave Owen, too. The thought makes my heart clench, but once I get my story, I'm done. I deserve better than to be stuck with this asshole.

CHAPTER NINE

Emma

M Y ENTIRE BODY HURTS SO FUCKING much and my head is clouded with both lust and never-ending questions. I've spent hours now on Owen's wolf's back, pressing my thighs against his massive form to hold on, gripping his black fur in my fists. It's dark now and getting cold. My back is freezing, but at least my face is warm, buried into Owen's back. Just when I think I can't hold on much longer, from too much exhaustion and fatigue, he starts to slow. My eyes pop open and I search the area in front of us to figure out where we're going to stay. I look to my left as I cautiously lift my head and see Luke in his wolf form. He's a beautiful beast, but fuck him. I can't fucking stand to look at him right now. I thought to be someone's mate meant to love them. But Luke doesn't seem to know the meaning of the word.

Instead I look straight ahead and my eyes widen. I don't really know what I expected. But not this.

It's a town. A very quirky town. The town you'd think of if you imagined a fairytale village. Yes, village. Village is a better description. With houses of different shapes and sizes and stone pathways connecting the small and large dwellings. All the houses appear to be made of stone and mortar, some with wood planked roofs, others with tin.

Owen and Luke slow their stride as we come closer to the village. They nod their heads slightly as children run past us, squealing with delight and chasing one another. I start to think that the line of small houses to my left can't possibly be real homes, they must be playhouses for the children. But then a row of foxes emerges and bows to my Alphas. Their bright red fur nearly blends in with their homes, but the tuft of white at the end of their fluffy tails and their white paws stand out against the red brick.

Foxes? They're sentient? I've never in my life heard of fox shifters.

Up a rather steep hill straight ahead, past the homes and little market, is a thick forest, and I can just barely make out a stone wall behind the trees that separates the village from what looks like a castle. It's a true-to-life fairytale setting.

All the homes seem to circle around a large fire pit in the center of the town, where nearly a dozen people are gathered around the fire. Or shifters, I'm not sure what they are. But I'm positive that they're all naked, which reminds me of my own state of undress. I shift uncomfortably on Owen's back in an attempt to cover myself, but he must take it as a sign that I want him to put me down.

Nope. Nope, that's not at all what I want. I shield my breasts and whisper to him, "I'm naked." Luke's wolf chortles on my left, which makes me narrow my eyes at him with even more contempt than I held for him just moments ago. The large white wolf's eyes spark with a challenge and I watch in amazement as Luke shifts in front of me. My breath stills in my lungs as his large muscular form appears before my eyes and the sex God emerges from what was a magnificent wolf.

He stalks toward me, forcing a desire from me I wish I could deny while also making me cower on Owen's back.

"What was that, sugar? You looked like you had something to say?" I shake my head as a wave of arousal hits me with a vengeance. How the hell could my sore body want anything other than sleep right now? I hate that I'm so turned on by him. Fucking prick.

Luke sniffs the air and groans, palming his dick. "We've got to get you inside, sugar. You can meet everyone later."

His large hands wrap around my waist and lift me off Owen's back with ease. The breeze between my legs makes me close them instantly and attempt to cover myself as best as I can. Luke laughs again, the low chuckle is sexy as hell, but I still don't appreciate it. With his arm wrapping around me, he shields my body. I'm grateful for that at least and it's the only reason I allow him to touch me.

As we walk toward a house, I notice it's rather large but not much different from the other houses surrounding the large fire pit. The group of people go silent and watch us with obvious interest. I walk quickly between Luke and Owen to hide myself from the prying eyes while keeping my own cast down as my cheeks flame with embarrassment.

"Don't worry, sweetness. There's nothing wrong with being nude. No one is going to look at you like that."

My arms cross tighter over my breasts as I mumble under my breath, "I don't feel comfortable."

Both Luke and Owen seem to straighten their backs. "We'll get you clothes then. Charlotte has some clothes—"

Luke interrupts Owen's response. "We'll get you more, you won't fit in her clothes." What the fuck does that mean? I glance at him, feeling even more self-conscious, but he doesn't even turn his head to look at me. I let out a large huff of air that turns into a yawn as we enter the house. It's decorated modestly with a contemporary edge, but it is, without a doubt, a bachelor pad.

"Is this…home?" Owen nods a yes at my question while Luke continues through the room and down the hallway. I have no idea where he's going, but with him gone I feel like I can breathe a little easier. "Is there internet?" I can't imagine that there is, but they are tech gurus or whatever he said before.

Owen's smile widens. "Of course." He takes my

hand and leads me past the living room, through a *slightly* outdated kitchen and into an office in the back. Holy shit. This office is insane. There are eight large, flat-screened monitors on the wall with three desks in the center of the room facing the monitors.

"Why are there three desks?"

"One for Charlotte. But you can use whichever one you want." He speaks matter-of-factly and I get a sick feeling in my stomach. Who is Charlotte? "Or if you want your own, we can get you one."

Before I can ask who the fuck Charlotte is, Luke comes back into the room holding a plain white tee. He's still naked and the sight of his body makes me close my eyes to repress the sexual urges I have for him.

"No social media though. The Authority doesn't allow it." I stare straight into Owen's eyes and nod, but inside I've already decided that I'll be leaking this story. What's the worst that can happen?

"Put this on." Luke finally speaks and holds out the shirt for me to take. I put it to my nose and inhale his masculine, woodsy scent. I love the smell but hate that it's from him. It's disturbing how just the very smell of him can do such strong things to me.

"No clothes in the house." Owen yanks the shirt

from my hand and a look of pure rage crosses over Luke's face. "She needs to be bared to us at all times." Luke's brows raise at Owen's response; he obviously approves of his twin's reasoning. They both look at me and my heart stutters from the primitive hunger in their eyes.

"No." The word slips through my lips as my first line of defense to protect myself from them. Luke's expression is unaltered, still emotionless and hard. Owen doesn't try to hide his amusement.

"Why's that, sweetness?" His cocky smiles drops just slightly as he asks, "You aren't in need?"

"I'm tired and want to sleep"—my breath comes in panicked bursts—"and I don't want to be naked all the time."

Owen's amusement disappears at my words. "Why?" Luke continues to stand there, just watching me, almost glaring at me.

It takes everything in me to get any reason out, my head is so cloudy. "I want to be clothed…and have a sense of normalcy." *And I'm not going to sleep with Luke ever again.* My heart hammers in protest.

Luke's eyes flash as if he heard me and for a moment I feel a break between us.

"Wear whatever the fuck you want. It's time for

bed." Luke turns his back to me and stalks out of the room. I don't know where he plans on going, but I'm not fucking following.

Owen's jaw ticks as he looks down at the shirt in his hand. "I don't want you to wear this. At least not tonight." I bite the inside of my cheek as he cocks his head and lets his eyes roam down my body. His breathing comes in shallow breaths and desire is written all over his face.

"I want to feel your skin against mine. It will be good for our bond." His response seems genuine, and I allow what he's saying to register.

I'll cave on this issue, but only so I can escape to bed. I'm tired. I can already feel myself getting hot for him, but I haven't got it in me to take any more physical activity tonight. I nod my head. "For tonight, fine. I just want to go to bed though."

Surprise and disappointment are evident in Owen's expression as he takes in my words. It takes so long for him to respond that I start to grow anxious. "Bed it is then." Relief overwhelms my sore, tired body as his arm wraps around me and he pulls me into his side and leads me out of the room.

As we enter a bedroom at the back of the house, Luke tosses a pillow onto the left side of the bed and pulls the covers back. I stop at the entrance to the room and stare at him and then Owen.

"What's the matter? Aren't you tired?" Owen looks down at me with confusion.

I part my lips then slam them shut looking between the two men who are watching me expectantly. "I want my own room." Owen laughs at my request as if I'm joking and Luke stares back at me with what looks like anger.

"Why would you want that? You'll be needing us."

"I can come and get you if I need you." Desire sends a wave of need through me at his words. Fuck, I do need them, but I don't want them. I don't want to lead them on any more than I have to.

There's not a doubt in my mind; I've decided I'm going to be leaving as soon as I get what I came for. My emotions war with themselves at the decision. I need to keep myself in check so I can leave them when the time comes. Guilt aches in my chest, but as my eyes meet Luke's hard stare, the guilt vanishes. I think he hates that I'm his mate. How could I ever stay when that's how he makes me feel?

"We'll need you too, though." Owen kisses my hair and strokes my back gently, making me involuntarily lean into his hot, hard body. Then I realize his words and my eyes pop open. "You have no idea what your scent does to us." I look between the two men as the meaning of everything comes into clear focus.

"I'm tired and I don't want to."

Luke lays back in the bed and doesn't respond to me.

"Get your sweet ass in bed, you've got to rest up. After all you're only human and the last two days have been rough on you." Owen's words hurt me more than they should. So what if I'm human?

"What's wrong?" Owen asks when I don't move. The two of them are fucking clueless.

"Nothing." I pull back the covers and scoot myself onto the bed, on the very edge to be as far away from Luke as possible.

"I don't like you lying to me." Owen stalks over to the bed and crawls onto the mattress, forcing me to move to the center.

"I may be human, but I'm not weak." I can hear how pissed I am and I wish I could've just kept my mouth shut. Why should this bother me at all? Luke opens his eyes and rolls onto his side to stare at me. As if he's suddenly interested in me and actually wants to have a conversation. But he doesn't speak. I look at him for a moment, waiting for him to say something, but I get nothing. I roll onto my side with my back to him.

"No one said you were weak." Owen's eyes focus on Luke's, and I get the impression that he's lying to my face. They think I'm weak. Just another reason I have for leaving them in however many days. I swallow and settle my *weak* body on the bed and give myself a deadline. Realistically my editor wants the story in two days, but I'm not sure two days will be enough. Once the story hits, I'll need to have a way to get out of here and be far away before the shitstorm comes this way. I need to scout out the place and figure out what the hell I'm going to do. Formulate a plan of escape.

As my eyes start to drift, a large arm settles across my midsection and pulls my back into a hot, solid chest of muscle. I don't have enough energy to open my eyes and register what's going on. As the hand splays across my belly another cups my chin and warm lips kiss mine. I murmur into the sweet touch and fall peacefully asleep, forgetting what it was that I was supposed to be thinking about.

CHAPTER TEN

Emma

"**Y**OU'RE CHARLOTTE?" A BEAUTIFUL, yet curvy brunette with big blue eyes smiles at me. She's so tall, she must be a wolf. I return her smile although I'm less than confident, "You're a shifter aren't you?" Even though I'm the one dressed in only a shirt, she's the one who appears shy. She nods. "Yeah. I'm a shifter."

I wouldn't be in the hall if I didn't truly need a restroom. I woke up about a half an hour ago and immediately grabbed a shirt from a dresser in the corner of the room. I awoke alone and a bit groggy. My entire body is sore, and I just want to soak in a hot bath. I didn't get far down the hallway to snoop in search for bathroom before I ran into Charlotte. Thank God she's clothed, at least. After relieving myself, she's there waiting for me and walks me back down to the bedroom.

"I hear you prefer clothes too."

I already like her. "Yeah, naked isn't really something I'm used to." I follow Charlotte back to the bedroom and that sick feeling comes back to the pit of my stomach. I don't like that she knows where the bedroom is. I rub my arm and look out of the window, trying to gather the courage to ask. Oh, fuck it. What's it matter anyway? It's not like I'll be here long. "So you hang out with the Luke and Owen a lot?" It's not really a question, just a statement.

"Yes, I do the promotional work for the company." She gives me a tight smile. "They suck at marketing." She shakes her head. "How the hell they thought they'd be successful with no advertising is beyond me." Her eyes widen and she holds up her hand. "Don't get me wrong, they're smart and everything, but they really weren't thinking when it came to actually selling. They had no clue."

I respond for the sake of responding even though

all I can think about is how comfortable she is in their bedroom. "I totally understand."

She sits on the edge of the bed, and I'm surprised by the spike of jealousy that hits me. I suppose it's natural to be jealous of a woman who's slept with the men you're currently sleeping with, even if you are trying to stay emotionally detached and planning your exit. I swallow the lump growing in my throat.

"So you do the advertising." A thought resonates in me and I decide to take advantage of the situation. It's good for an *interviewee* to feel comfortable. I can get some information out of her. "So do all the shifters here work for the company. Is that how a pack works?"

The beautiful woman broadens her smile. "No, we do whatever we like, so long as we contribute a fair share. The foxes like to garden, so they make sure to plant enough vegetables for those who want them. And a few of the bears like to build the houses. The cats like to do the nitty gritty, like plumbing and electrical." I keep my mouth shut and try not to show my surprise. The foxes *were* shifters. Holy shit. We have foxes back home, they could easily be shifters and I would've had no clue. This is going to make such a good story. It will give us ammunition to demand more information about the shifters. The Authority keeps so much a secret it's fucking criminal.

"I'm not sure what everyone does exactly, but as long as the Alphas approve of their role, we don't question it. There's no reason to." Although this is all good information, I find myself focusing on the fact that she may or may not have slept with Owen and Luke. I shift my weight onto my left foot and decide to ask some questions to hint around it. I don't want to make an enemy of her.

"So I always thought shifters were monogamous."

She seems surprised by my confession, her brow arching. "Well, most are." She looks down and toys with the threads on the comforter. The comforter that I slept under with Luke and Owen. "Some species don't have fated mates, so they aren't—Like dragons. Dragons aren't known for mates at all anymore. But bears and wolves are, and cats prefer to be monogamous, but they don't always have fated mates, so you know. It doesn't always work." Her eyes go sad at the thought, but only for a moment. "And then some mates deny the connection. Which is just really awful."

"What do you mean?" That sick feeling in the pit of my stomach grows.

"About what?"

"About denying mates." I hope I'm not giving her the impression that denying them is exactly what I plan on doing.

"Oh, well from how I understand it, it's the animal part of the shifter that feels the connection. So long as the human and animal are on the same page, it's easy to feel their mate. But if they aren't, they could miss their mate or feel it, but not give in to the pull. And then there are instances where one person doesn't feel the connection and denies their mate's animal of their partner and it completely wrecks the animal."

"Wrecks the animal?" I question as my blood pressure rises.

"Yeah like, sometimes they lose their ability to shift altogether. Or an Alpha who has a mate, like Owen and Luke having you, well they get more powerful, stronger, and their ability to use their dominance over others grows. But if they're denied, they become weaker. So it's fantastic that Owen and Luke found you!" Her voice is all peppy at the end as she fills with excitement.

"But they aren't monogamous." Suddenly I find myself hoping that she has fucked them. It would give me a good push to leave and forget the fact that I would be hurting them simply by leaving. Their wolves will get weaker, but that doesn't seem *that* bad.

She tilts her head and gets a sad look in her eyes. "They aren't? Why would they do such a thing?"

"I just assumed." I close my eyes; the weight of her response denies that she's been with them.

"Well as far as anyone here knows, they've only ever been with you." She scrunches her nose. "And I can tell you I've never smelled them on anyone else before."

I heat with embarrassment and bite my lip. "Are all you wolves good at smelling?"

She laughs at my irritation. "I'm not a wolf, but most shifters are good at smelling."

"What are you?"

"Lion."

"So you can shift into a lioness?"

She smiles and nods. "I don't much though."

"Why?"

"She's a bit aggressive. It's rare that a female possesses so much dominance. I try to repress her, but she doesn't like it when I do. So I just don't shift much."

"I don't understand. That sounds awful."

Her tone drops slightly, almost uncomfortably so.

"Well when dominance is expressed, it's challenged. For a female surrounded by stronger males, especially males who aren't her mate, that's not good for her." She offers me a sad smile. "It's why I left my pride."

"Oh my God, they didn't—" I can't even finish my thought, but she adamantly shakes her head, stopping any assumptions from turning dark.

"No, my family would never hurt me. But my lioness kept picking fights and would sulk when she would be beat in a match. It was just too much for both of us to handle. I think she wants to be tamed, but only by her mate. And I haven't found him yet. We were both miserable, so I left, hoping to find my mate." She shakes her head. "But after a year, I never found him so I just stopped looking." She looks sad but resigned. "A lot of shifters never find their mates. When you get to a point in your life, you just have to make a decision of whether you'd rather have a small bond with someone else, or no bond at all."

My eyes search hers. "What did you decide?"

"I haven't made my decision yet, but I'm getting to the point where I need to." My heart aches for her as she changes the subject, not so subtly. "Ooh I can smell your heat hitting you." She wrinkles her nose comically.

"So heat means what exactly?" I find myself sitting on the bed beside her. All of this is exactly what I was hoping for. My fingers itch to snag my recorder but I resist on the off chance that she'll stop giving intel if she knows my intention.

"It's the time of the month when you're most fertile." I nod my head and immediately feel like an idiot for not figuring that one out on my own. Heat…like a dog. "And shifters get super, forgive my bluntness, horny around that time."

"Well good thing I'm human." I don't expect her to laugh, but oh she does and I find my face heating.

"You aren't feeling horny at all? From what I've heard it hits humans just as hard and sometimes harder."

I sit uncomfortably on the bed, tug down the tee shirt, and feel the ache between my thighs. *Oh shit…* I remember Luke's remark about begging him and I hope it's not true. I won't be able to handle that. Being so degraded and having no control over it. "Maybe I should stay with someone else until the heat's over."

She looks at me like I've lost my mind. "Why would you want that?" She doesn't wait for a reply, instead she just shakes her head. "The Alphas won't allow that so I wouldn't suggest it. They aren't going to be able to let their mate be anywhere but with them. No mate would ever want their partner somewhere without them during their heat. It's awfully painful to be apart." Before I can reply she adds, "And I'm sure they're going to want to bond with you before the claiming."

A cold sweat breaks across my skin as my gut drops. "What's the claiming?" Every inch of my skin tingles.

"For wolves it's when they bite you, to mark you as theirs." I nod my head. Okay, that doesn't sound so bad. "The bite lets their magic mix with your blood. That way everyone will scent you as theirs and they'll always be able to find you and know how you're feeling. It's wonderful." Her tone and smile brighten once again. "And the claiming moon is only four days away."

Fuck. I need to get the hell out of here in less than four days.

CHAPTER ELEVEN

Luke

I STIFLE MY GROAN AS ANOTHER WAVE OF HER arousal hits me, the entire house smells of her sweet honey. She hasn't sought either of us out today and that confuses me. We waited close by, not even daring to leave the house. I know the pack wants to meet her, but they understand what a test it would be for all of us at this point. Even having Charlotte in the house put us on edge. There's no fucking way that she'd ever be interested in our sweet little mate, but still. I don't want anyone around her.

We've only had a single interaction with Emma today. Maybe it's because she's human… I'm not sure.

She almost left the house, she didn't even come to see us first, like she was purposely avoiding us.

She's obviously upset with us for keeping her inside, but she doesn't understand. Owen is the one who spoke up when she objected, and she hasn't said a word to him since. I'm hoping that means she'll want me first. I've been waiting all day. We both have. I didn't get a damn thing done. We're behind on work since we took an extra two days getting back here to round up our mate. We also have to alert the Authority to the fact that we found our mate and she's a human. I'm not looking forward to explaining that, not that I could at this moment anyway. I can't concentrate for shit. We're both eager for her. Both pining over her and waiting for her to need us.

The light of day has faded and it's time to confront our little mate. We've stayed in the office for the most part of the day. She has had plenty of time to get adjusted, and Charlotte helped her as we asked her to. Emma's mostly just been scribbling in that damn notebook of hers all day. Each time I came to check on her, she didn't even bother looking up from that book. I've got to take a peek as soon as I can. I want to know everything about her. *My mate.*

Just as I leave the office to tend to her, Owen

walks up on my left and starts to head to the bedroom. Irritation claws at me. He had her last and I need to feel her under me and for her to feel our bond. The way things ended our first time was not at all what I wanted.

I'd planned on holding her and soothing her. My fists clench as a memory of her pushing away from me hits me. I'd planned on giving her exactly what Owen gave her. The memory of her crying out his name hits me harder than I thought it would. I know he's her mate as well, but it felt like nothing but betrayal. I may have had her first, but he had a completely different piece that matters just as much. And I've yet to have that with her.

I know she's less than happy with me because of it. But I'll give her what she needs and make up for being jealous and crass. She'll learn how I am. I've never been good with my words or emotions. As anxiousness and fear that she'll deny me in favor of my brother creep up, I promise myself I'll be more careful with her. Besides, Owen didn't love her like I did. My brows furrow looking at my brother. I don't understand why he's so forceful with her. I mean, fuck, he denied her. She wanted to come and he made her wait. I'd never do that. *You'll take what I give you.* His words make my wolf snarl. I'd be more pissed if she didn't seem to like it as much as she does.

I've never felt such insecurity. Truth be told, I wish we didn't have to share her. She will compare us, and Owen's always been the good one.

I plan on giving her the fucking world, to spoil her. Anything she wants, she gets. Even if Owen objects. It pisses me off that he overrules me. Like with that fucking tee shirt. We need to sit down and have a conversation about that. But right now, we've got to figure out who's going in there first. Her heat is driving us mad.

"You had her last." My hand comes down hard on his shoulder, preventing him from leaving the office. A low growl grows in his chest as he turns around. This is really going to get ugly as the claiming moon approaches if we don't figure out how to handle this. I'm ready to throw down again, but I don't want to. Not when our pack will know. Not when they haven't met our mate yet, and how we behave will reflect on her. He's my brother, my other half for so long. And she seems to enjoy him too. An image of her screaming his name as she came on his dick flashes before my eyes. Instead of the anger I expect, a hurt settles deep in my chest. I clear my throat. "It's only fair."

He looks me dead in the eyes as his fists clench. "Together."

"Not fucking happening." No fucking way. I may have to share her, but after last time, I don't want to watch. I don't want to see anyone else giving her pleasure. I don't want to hear her saying his name. I want her to love me. Me. I want her to feel me and our bond and our connection. She felt it with him. I know she did. And he interrupted us before she could feel it with me.

"You've bonded…we have not," I tell him bluntly, unable to contain a tinge of concern in my tone. He curses under his breath before conceding.

"You take her ass and I'll beat the shit out of you."

I shake off every apprehension as soon as I'm out of that office and head straight toward that sweet scent. My dick is so hard I leak precum before I even open the door. I can't wait to have her lick it off and clean me up before I get dirty again. The thought makes my dick jump. I stroke it once and try to gather my composure.

If I didn't keep myself in check, I'd hurt her. I know I would. It's the only reason I had to keep an eye on Owen as he took her. He doesn't care that she's human and that's going to get her hurt. She can't handle us. I'm just waiting for that horrific moment when one of us takes it too far. The very thought makes my heartbeat slow and my hands go numb. I shake them out and get my shit together. Ready to please my mate.

As soon as I see her I know something's wrong. She's lying on the bed but gripping the sheets. The covers have been kicked all the way to the bottom of the bed. Her eyes are closed tight and she's panting like she's just had a tiring run through the woods. Her legs are closed, knees bent, and she rocks them back and forth. I silently close the door behind me and stalk over to her. She's fighting her heat? A strangled moan is barely audible. I want to reach out and touch her, but I'm afraid I'll startle her too much. She's not even close to being coherent.

I lick my lips before quietly asking, "You all right, sugar?" Her eyes pop open and she grips the sheets tighter, digging her nails into the bed.

"I'm fine." Her nostrils flare as she answers at me through clenched teeth.

"You don't look fine. You look like you may need me? You want—" I gently place my hand on her stomach, ready to rub that little nub of hers and get her off to give her some relief. Although she needs me inside her before her heat will calm, her hand flies down, smacking me away as she jackknifes off the bed.

"Fuck you! I won't beg you for anything!" The look she's giving me would make a lesser wolf cower. Who said anything about begging? At first I'm confused and then I remember that shit I said when we were back in the woods. Fucking hell.

After running a hand down my face, I stare back at her and watch her anger slip as her heat takes possession of her again. She falls against the mattress with her fists closed tightly and lays on her side in the fetal position. She's got to be in pain. The sight of her makes my wolf whine in agony.

"I don't want you to beg me sugar, just let—"

She cuts me off. "Owen! I want Owen!" The breath leaves my lungs and my legs nearly give out. My heart stills and my wolf cowers in shame. My mate denied me. A numbness takes over my body as an emptiness fills my chest. She's in need. But she won't let me please her. Have I hurt her that bad? I open my mouth, but no words come out. Instead I swallow and give myself a moment. Clenching and unclenching my fists. I've never felt so powerless in my life. She moans, but not in pleasure, she's in pain.

I feel tears prick and that's not going to fucking

happen. I'm an Alpha. I'm not going to cry. I'm sure as fuck not going to let her see how weak I am. She will never love me then if she sees how vulnerable I am to her emotions toward me. Instead I nod, not that she sees, and turn on my heels to leave. Forcing myself to leave her.

Pain tears through me when I open the door.

Owen's standing right fucking there. I know he heard everything. He looks torn up. He looks exactly how I feel. It pisses me off; she didn't do that shit to him. She fucking asked for him. He has no right to look at me like that.

I snarl as I pass him, avoiding this shit and the possibility that he would see me like this. I hear him open the door as I slam the bathroom door open. Fuck! The damn thing comes off its hinges and blocks my way to the sink. I kick it, splintering the wood. I grab a piece and throw it against the wall, growling as it cracks the drywall and smashes against the tiled floor. Adrenaline courses through my veins, fueling my anger.

Anger I can deal with. Anger is an emotion I can handle. But even as I cling to the anger, to the rage that Owen would pity me and our mate would choose him over me, I feel the hopelessness overwhelming me. My wolf lies helpless, not bothering to contribute anything. I grip the edge of the ceramic sink to keep myself balanced. After a moment to get my shit together, I turn on the faucet and splash my face with water. I look into the mirror and see an asshole staring back. I hurt her. I didn't realize how much my words affected her. I can make it up to her. I'll just apologize. Fuck, I really am fucking sorry. I can be such a stupid prick. But all I need to do is apologize. That's it. I wipe my face, assuring myself that will be enough. I just need her to know how much I care for her and apologize for being an ass. It would have been better had I said nothing. I knew better. I'll do better.

My breath comes back slowly and my blood cools from the tormented simmer. I crack my neck and my shoulders and look around at the mess I made. Fuck, I'll clean it up later. I'm not waiting for Owen to leave her. He probably won't move from her side any way. I'll just wait until there's a moment for me to enter and then I'll go in and apologize.

I shake out my shoulders and head toward the bedroom. I have to close my eyes and breathe deep as I hear her moan. It fucking shreds me. She whimpers my brother's name. I take a hesitant step forward. Wondering if I can really do this. Can I listen to someone else giving my mate pleasure even if he is her mate as well? I hear the bed banging rhythmically against the wall. It's not loud. So he's not being too rough with her. I run my hands down my face and breathe out heavily. Fuck, just the thought of him on top of her, rutting into her. My hands tremble so I fist them to make the shaking stop.

I just need to listen and wait. I shake my head and turn around. I'll come back in an hour. No! Fuck, I need to man the fuck up and listen so I know when I can go to her. I fucking hurt her, I can deal with this shit. It's my punishment. I walk back to the door and stop with my hand on the doorknob. My fingers close tightly around it, refusing to turn the knob.

I know he's her mate. I should be grateful that it's my brother and not some other asshole. But fuck, I can't stand the thought of him pleasuring her.

"Harder," she screams as though she's in pain. The sound of him pounding into her tempts my beast to fight him. I grit my teeth to keep myself from barging in and ripping his fucking throat out. I roll my shoulders and open the door.

I slowly walk into the room and watch as my brother's body hovers over Emma. Her fingernails pierce into his back. Small red scratches line his back.

Her heels dig into his ass. I close my eyes, but that only makes it worse. Her moans and the sound of him rocking his body into her, the bed hitting the wall. I nearly turn away, but I make myself take another step toward her. Her breathing is picking up; his breathing is ragged. As soon as she's sated I'll go to her. He suggested we take her together. Maybe with him there and me apologizing. Maybe then she'll want me too.

My jaw ticks as he nips at her neck and pushes himself deep inside her heat, making her cry out as her orgasm hits her. I know he's coming inside her. He may sire her first pup. All because I was a fucking ass and couldn't keep my mouth shut. My hands run down my face and I clench my jaw. Waiting for their embrace to end. He's kissing her jaw as she hums in satisfaction. I take a step toward them, willing my body to approach and take my mate any way I can.

"Owen. Owen." She mewls under him as after-shocks rock through her body. "I love you, Owen." Those words on her lips make me question every-thing. *She loves him.* She loves my brother. I turn quickly and leave, hoping neither of them saw me.

She doesn't want me.

She doesn't love me.

Only my brother.

CHAPTER TWELVE

Owen

"**F**UCK!" I SLAM THE PHONE DOWN AND stare at Luke. He hasn't said a fucking word to me since last night. I hate being on bad terms with him. It's even worse knowing I've got to leave him to go handle this shit.

"What?" He doesn't even look up from the computer.

"I've been summoned." He stops typing but still doesn't look at me. "They want to meet in person to discuss our partnership."

"The vampires are a silent partner. What's there to discuss?" He sounds disinterested, but he's merely tapping a single key over and over, not typing, just waiting to hear what I have to tell him.

"There are other aspects of our deal." That gets his attention. Finally his eyes meet mine. His hard expression reflects the anger and nervousness I'm doing my best to contain.

"What the fuck do they want?"

"They won't answer over the phone."

"What are you thinking?"

"No fucking clue, but it must be something big for them to summon us."

"Us? No fucking way. Only one of us goes." We stare hard at each other. I clench my jaw so hard I hear something crack. "We can't leave her and we sure as fuck can't bring her." He casts his eyes down and turns away from me. "I'll go. You stay with her." My chest pains at the sight of him. He's so fucking beat up that she turned him away yesterday. I don't know why she did it. She wouldn't answer me when I asked. She wouldn't let me leave but wouldn't talk to me. She wouldn't let me get him. I imagined this may be difficult for her but I didn't expect her to… to be so willfully distant. I'm grateful she didn't deny me. I can't imagine what Luke is feeling.

I expected him to come in last night. I thought

he'd try again to win her approval. "Stop fucking moping. You should be ashamed of yourself."

"I am." He starts typing again and I know he's trying to ignore me. Anger gets the best of me as I rise out of my seat.

"That's not what I meant." I rip the keyboard out of his hands and throw it on the ground. It shatters and I can tell it pisses him the fuck off, but I don't give a shit. "You're just going to give up on your mate?"

"It's not giving up." His eyes find mine and I can tell he's only holding on by a thread. "I'm giving her what she wants."

It fucking kills me to see him like this. Even if he weren't my brother, knowing what we went through, what he went through… "Fuck, Luke."

"What the fuck do you want from me?" He screams at me, pounding on his chest. The action rouses his wolf. It's the first time my wolf has felt his all day.

I stress my answer although it should be obvious. "Not to give up on her."

He looks at me like I'm his enemy and a cold chill runs through me. "She wants you, not me. She's made that clear."

I spear my fingers through my hair and watch Luke as he stands to leave. "You have to stay." My words keep him from leaving. It takes a moment for him to face me again. He looks like the shell of the man he was just yesterday. "You look like shit and your wolf is silent. You'll look weak to them." My words hurt me just as much as they hurt him. A sickness churns in my gut watching my once strong and proud brother turn inward. "I don't think she realizes what she's doing. She's just scared of what she feels or something. Heat can be hard on the best of us, and she's only just come into this world."

Luke nods his head and tries to speak but doesn't. His eyes fall and I can see his inner war. "It's not over Luke." His sad eyes find mine and I feel guilty as fuck. "You stay with her. Try. Just try."

"It fucking hurts, Owen." Luke's hand rubs against his chest. I've never seen my brother so disheveled and wretched. I pull him in for a quick hug and pound on his back.

"You can't just let her go." I can't believe he would even consider leaving our mate.

"I'm not. She's with you." Luke pulls away from me and stares down the hallway. "At first, I thought I'd kill you." He looks back at me with no remorse although his eyes rolling indicates he's aware of how ridiculous the thought is. "I literally thought, for the smallest of moments, I should kill you." His words should chill my blood but they don't. "Then I thought, I can't do that to you, you're my brother, and she would only hate me more because she loves you." He slams his fist on the door frame. "But then I realized the truth"—he swallows thickly—"I couldn't do it, because it would hurt her." His tortured eyes find mine. "It would hurt her to take away someone she loved."

I stare back at my twin with nothing to say. I wish I could take this pain away from him, but I can't. Only Emma can.

"I haven't given up." Hearing him admit he still has hope relaxes me, but only slightly. He clears his throat. "I won't ever stop trying. Just trying to get my wolf on board." Knowing his wolf is leaving him fucking kills my own animal. "You tell her. I'm going on a short run; I don't want to hear what she thinks about it." He slams a hand on my back. "Let me know what they say and make sure you take the Betas."

I watch my brother leave and I can't get over the feeling of sickness in my chest. I need to talk to

Emma and tell her just how torn up he is. But then she may think he's weak. Shit. I don't know what to do. I don't want her to think of him as any less of a man, a wolf, an Alpha. He's my equal. Different, yeah. But he'd be just as good a mate to her as I would. Together we can give her everything. Just as we have our pack. I lean against the wall on my forearms and let out a tortured sigh. He's going to have to win her over on his own. At least now I have a reason to give them time alone together.

I gather my thoughts and push off the wall, I need to tell my mate I'm leaving. I should be leaving right now, but I at least need to tell her that I'm going. There's a small chance that I'll get into some shit heading out there. It's small, but still, I need to tell her.

Heading to the bedroom, I don't make it more than a few steps before taking another scent of the air. My brows furrow and I look down the hall with confusion. I walk over to the window and lift it up, staring down into the dirt. I see where she landed. What the fuck is my mate doing jumping out the window? Then reality slams into my chest. She's sneaking out. My mate fucking snuck out. She left us. While in heat!

It doesn't take long to scent her in the woods up to the abandoned estate. What the fuck is she doing up here? I hear the clang of the gate and tick my jaw. It won't open for her. It hasn't opened in nearly a hundred years. Only the magic that left the forest once the spell of the beast was broken will open the gate. I stalk to my mate and watch as her tiny fingers trace the intricate detail. She flashes a camera before putting it in her bag and looking behind her. Checking to see if anyone is following her. I huff and press my lips together. She takes a phone out of her rather stuffed backpack. A look of disappointment crosses her face before she holds the phone up into the air checking for a signal.

Anger consumes me. She asked about contacting people, I told her she couldn't. The Authority would be on her in minutes, and I'm not prepared to take on their fucking army with this small pack.

"What are you doing, sweetness?" My harsh voice startles her and she drops the phone. She looks back at me with wide eyes. Frozen in place. The weight of the moment hits me. She's really trying to leave me. Leave us. My fingers go numb, but I stalk my way to her, and she stays perfectly still.

She doesn't answer, she only looks up at me with wide eyes as I close the distance between us.

She denies my brother, confesses her love for me, and then tries to leave us both? My arm wraps around her lower back and I lean down to kiss her. Showing her affection allows her guard to come down. Even as I kiss her, I scent the air and I'm all too aware her heat is waning. I hold her lips with mine, savoring this moment. Knowing it could be our last. My wolf claws my chest, whining, refusing to allow it to happen. But if she truly wants to leave. I can't stop her. I won't do that to her. I won't let her think she has to stay with us. I need her to *want* to stay with us. I won't make her a prisoner.

"I was just going to tell you I had to leave for a day or two. I have to go to a meeting and it can't be put off." I speak into her hair, smelling her vanilla scent and memorizing it. I'll never stop watching over her and keeping her out of harm's way. And killing any fucker that tries to lay a hand on her. I shake my head. I can't think like that right now. I can still convince her to stay. If it doesn't work, I'll just have to keep trying. My wolf howls in agony and I ignore him.

I finally pull away from her and run my fingers

down her jaw, down her throat. I rub a soothing circle in the crook of her neck where I imagined my claiming mark would be. "I see you were planning on leaving me first." Guilt flashes in her eyes. "You didn't even say goodbye." My voice is calm and steady; like she didn't just rip my heart out of my chest.

"I—" I put a finger over her lips before she can lie to me.

"Why are you leaving us?" I let my voice go cold. At least she looks just as fucking tore up as I feel.

"I can't stay here."

"Why the fuck not?" My voice comes out harder than I want it to, but I can't change that.

"I can't stay here." Her eyes cast down and she whispers, "with him."

I stare at her, unable to truly believe what she's saying. I've heard of mates being denied, but it's rare. While I'm concerned about Luke, I also can't help the feeling of hope that lingers in my tight chest. Maybe she'll only leave him; maybe she'll stay with me. I close my eyes and curse myself for being such a selfish prick, but she is my mate.

"I'll be gone for a day, two at most. Stay with him until then." She starts to protest, but I talk over her, finishing the thought. "If you want to leave when I get home, I'll take you back." Saying the words crumples my chest and makes my wolf snarl with denial. I don't know if the words are true. I don't know if I could actually let her leave, but I need to give her this so she'll stay just a little longer.

Her eyes, glossy with tears, stare into mine. I don't know what she's searching for in order to agree, but I fucking hope she finds it. She nods her head, looking solemn and resolved to leave us. She turns her body toward the village, ready to leave me, but I'm not ready to leave her. I'll be gone and the moment I get home she may be ready to leave, or worse, she may have already left. I just need one more moment with her.

"I should punish you for this." I growl the words in her ear. My dick hardens at the thought. I remember the way it felt when she pushed against me. When I first touched her and felt the spark, the pull to her, the need for her. I place my hand around her neck and run my thumb down her throat. "What do you think Emma? Do you want to leave me now? Do you want to run from me?"

I'm playing with fire. Pushing her like this. But fuck I want it. Let her try to run from me. I'll catch her and pin her to the ground like I've fantasized. Her eyes haze with lust knowing exactly what I want from her.

"You want me to run?" Her breathy voice makes my wolf howl with need.

"I want you to tell me to stop." She looks at me with confusion. But I need this. I need to know that I won't cross the line. "Say it now."

"Stop." She barely speaks the word and I move closer to her, crowding her space.

"Say it again."

"Stop." She speaks clearly this time.

"Good girl." I kiss the dip in her throat. "I'm going to punish you, but I want you to enjoy this." I kiss her lips gently. "If you want me to stop." I kiss her neck. "All you need to do it say the word." I lean back, wanting to ensure that she understands.

"Okay." Her answer is breathy. Even if she wants to leave, she still wants me. At least once more.

"If it gets too much?"

"I'll say stop."

"Good girl. Now try running from me, sweetness." I move my hand to the back of her head and lean down to give her a gentle kiss, before nipping her lip. "Just try running and see how I'll punish you. It's what I should be doing to you right now." I pull away slowly, watching her dark eyes spark with desire. The smell of her arousal floods my lungs. Maybe she'll allow us for the sake of relief from her heat. Afterall, now that her body knows us, she'll feel this way every heat. She'll need us. I cling to the hope that it will be enough. As soon as my hand drops to my side, she bolts. I watch her duck in between trees and run away from me, deeper into the forest. It hurts something deep inside me, but I push it aside and run after my mate.

My heavy strides crush everything in my path. I don't bother letting her get far. I need to be inside her. I need to feel her body against me. I want nothing more than to hear her moaning my name and telling me that she loves me again. I grab her small waist and wrap my arms around her body as she fights against my hold. I easily pin her body down and put my teeth to her neck. Another wave of her heat hits me as I rock my erection between her slit, feel her honey coat my dick. It's far too easy to push the shirt above her hips and feel her soft body under mine.

She pushes against me as I nudge my dick into her heat and growl the words I desperately need to say while breathing into her neck, "Don't you ever fucking think about leaving me again." Before she can respond, before she can even truly register my words, I slam into her to the hilt and rut violently into her warmth. I'm desperate for her pleasure. I need her to come on my dick just as much as I need to come inside of her. I pound into her. I'm fueled by my need to claim her.

I'm struck by a thought that makes me eager to come. I growl with triumph as I ruthlessly fuck my mate in the dirt. My hands grip her ass and tilt her up so I hit her clit with every downward stroke. My fingers dig into her hips as her back arches off the ground.

I pound into her, slamming to the hilt each time. I grab her throat and squeeze, not enough to bruise her or to cut off oxygen, but enough to show her my strength and pin her there. With one hand on her hip and the other on her throat, I watch as her body jolts with each hard, merciless thrust. Fucking hell, she's gorgeous like this. A flush rising up her chest, her sultry eyes staring into mine. It doesn't take long for her pussy to clamp down on my dick, while her head falls back and she screams out in pleasure. The image of her overwhelmed with the pleasure I gave her is all I need. I come instantly.

"I love you, Owen." She turns her head to the side, trying to hide herself as she starts to cry. It shreds me. She moves away from me the moment she can, leaving me wanting. "I'm so sorry. I love you."

The moment is over before its begun. Her sorrow is a knife to my heart. I know she loves me; she doesn't need to say it.

"I love you, Emma." I kiss her hair and hold her to my chest, hoping she knows just how much she means to me. Thank God she lets me hold her.

I've never lived without my brother; I can't imagine taking his mate away from him. Making him leave or leaving with his mate, either option would be akin to killing him myself. But how could I let my mate leave me? If he doesn't win her over, I don't know what the fuck I'm going to do.

CHAPTER THIRTEEN

I'm so torn and confused. My heart's twisted in my chest. Aching with the need to stay with Owen. I was prepared to leave them behind and go back to my old life. I have enough information to make a decent manuscript. There's so much more to learn, but I can't risk staying any longer. I can't risk them claiming me. The heat is hard enough. I can barely think straight with it.

I do know one thing though; I'm falling hard for Owen. I know he already has my heart. But I can't come between him and his brother. I don't see myself with Luke. Ever. I don't care that I'm his mate. I just can't be with someone who thinks so little of me. Like I'm just expected to spread my legs for him. I'll never beg someone to love me.

Owen's already left. He said it will only be a day or two, but this fucking heat is killing me. I'm primed for another orgasm, already missing his touch. Every second seems to raise the threshold of pleasure. I close my eyes and grip the sheets harder, trying to repress the aching need between my legs. I tried satisfying myself before, which only made me more desperate for their touch. The sound of the door makes me open my eyes.

Luke.

I stare at the rugged man in front of me and the very sight of him makes my heart twist in agony. He looks the same, dark and intense, but his eyes are mournful. The dominance and power that were so much a part of his image no longer exist. I fist the sheets tighter, resisting the urge to touch him. A base need deep inside me pleads with me to comfort him. I agreed to stay here. But I have no intention of giving any more of myself to him.

"You're in pain." I keep my eyes closed, ignoring how fucking sexy his voice is. How the deep rumble of it soothes the anger in me.

"I'm fine." I say it with as flat of a voice as I'm able, but it manages to come out needy.

"You aren't." I feel the bed dip and hear the sound of it softly creak a few feet away. "I'm sorry."

I'm sure he is. He's sorry I didn't beg him. I keep my snide remark to myself.

"I didn't mean to hurt you. I didn't realize—" I open my eyes as he sighs and covers his face with his hands. He moves them to his lap and looks at me with such guilt it's hard to deny that he means every word.

He swallows thickly as his sad eyes find mine. "I know you love him. I won't come between you two. Let me just ease you for now. And when he comes back, I'll leave. I won't come back. I won't stand in the way of mates." A chill of despair washes through me and I shake my head, denying that I love Owen, denying the very truth he speaks. I don't want to love him. I don't want to love either of them. Not when I plan to leave as soon as I'm able.

"I heard you. I heard everything." He spears his fingers in his hair, the same way that Owen does, and places a gentle hand on my thigh. My body sparks at the simple touch and I feel an intense urge to lean into him and rub against his body. "I know what the heat does, and I won't take advantage. My needs will be my own to take care of. Just let me take the pain away."

A lump grows in my throat as I watch him slowly stalk toward me. His inhales are low and deep, as though his chest hurts him by simply breathing. I thought I knew exactly who he was and what he thought of me. But the man sitting on the bed with me is nothing like the Luke I'd conjured in my head.

"I don't know what to say." I'm confused and tears unwillingly leave me. I don't understand the emotions laying heavy on my heart.

"I love you, Emma. I'll always care for you. But I understand that you don't feel the same toward me." My eyes blur with tears as I watch him take my hand in his. "I wish you may one day want to give me another chance. And if you ever decide you could love us both, I'll come for you." He kisses the back of my hand and then turns it over to kiss my wrist.

"I'll be here for you. If you need me to take away the pain. Just let me know." He takes another deep breath and slowly rises to leave me.

A hole gashes my heart watching him. I know he could be lying and I should keep my guard up. I've met assholes like him who will say anything they can to get what they want. That's what this is. It must be.

I bet he's lying about not using me for his own needs too. Well, two can play that game. I'm in desperate need and I'm willing to give him the chance to prove me wrong. Not that I think he will.

"Please," I finally speak, just as he reaches the door. He quickly turns and I second guess my opinion of him when I see the hope in his eyes.

"Please what, Emma?"

"Please make it stop."

"What do you want me to do?" Honestly, I don't give a fuck. I just need this sensation to leave me. I can't stand this heat that makes my body shake with need. I'm on the very edge of my release and it's all I can think about. Swallowing thickly, I shake my head unable to think, and as though he understands, he settles between my thighs and pushes two large fingers into me and strokes against my g-spot. The pleasure is instant but still not enough. My body hums at the simple touch and I fall heavy against the mattress as my body gives in to the indulgence. He pinches my clit, and that's all I need to take me over. A slow wave of pleasure rocks through my body. His touch leaves me as aftershocks make my entire body quiver. All too soon it's over and the need to come again hits me instantly, frustrating the hell out of me. My head thrashes from side to side as my hands cover my face. I just want it to stop. Tears leak out of the corner of my eyes. It hurts too much.

The need slowly subsides as Luke's warm tongue gently licks my core. "Better?" he asks, lifting his head only slightly. My hands grip his hair as a frustrated moan leaves me and I push myself back onto his tongue. My eyes pop open, realizing how desperate I've shown myself to be, and I expect him to laugh. Instead, he suckles my clit into his mouth and continues finger fucking me. I lay my head back and moan into the warm air. I'm vaguely aware that I'm pushing my pussy into his face, wanting more, needing more.

I need him. Just as the thought hits me, I get pissed. He's doing this to me. He's *making* me need more by keeping me on edge. Just like Owen did when we first made love. But Luke isn't doing it to make anything feel more intense. He's doing it so I'll ask him to fuck me. So I'll *beg* him. The pain is unimaginable. Of course that's what he's doing. That's what he wants. It doesn't matter though, I'm going to leave. I *have* to leave. I can't stay here. So what does it matter?

I remember our first time. He took my virginity. I gave him that. I swallow the lump in my throat as another orgasm threatens to paralyze my body.

I'll let him have me beg. I'll pretend he loves me. I want it so bad. I want him to love me. But I'm a fool to think that he ever will. He's not the kind of man who loves a woman. I can pretend though. Like he's pretending now.

"I need you Luke." I wipe the corner of my eyes and watch as he licks his lips, glistening with my arousal.

"Please don't tempt me, sugar." I melt at his words. He's good at this. At pretending he's doing this for me. I'll drop my walls just enough to believe it. But only for the moment.

"Please love me, Luke." I don't realize the words I've spoken until they've escaped my lips. He's on me in an instant. Kissing up my body, my neck. Taking my lips hungrily with his. I taste myself on his tongue and moan into his mouth as he rocks his hard dick against my pussy.

"Tell me what you want me to do."

"Please fuck me Luke." I say the words and a piece of me breaks. He told me I'd beg and I did. I push it down. *This is just make-believe.* It doesn't make me any less of a woman to play out this fantasy.

"No." His hard word catches me off guard. "*Tell me* what you want."

I stare at him. His eyes shine with hope and desire. His breath is ragged. I obey my Alpha. "Fuck me, Luke."

He slams into me the moment the words are spoken. A strangled cry leaves me as my pussy pulses around his dick. He doesn't still in me, doesn't give me time to adjust to his size. He fucks me with a primitive need, pounding relentlessly into me with a steady, hard pace. I moan into the crook of his neck as another orgasm approaches. My body heats and chills as waves of pleasure slowly numb my body in a slow, pulsing rhythm. Each wave more intense that the last.

He kisses and nips my neck. I tilt my head to give him more of me. "I love you, Emma." His warm breath on my neck sends shivers down my body. My heels dig into his ass as my body comes off the bed and my orgasm racks through me. I feel his hot release inside me and instinctually expose my throat to him. A spark ignites between us. A pull so violent and primitive that I fear its strength. *I love you, Emma.* His voice echoes in my head as aftershocks make me tremble beneath him. I feel his lips on my neck and imagine devotion. As though he's worshipping my body.

It's only a fairytale, this isn't real. He's giving me

what I want only so he can get what he wants. He doesn't truly love me. He can't.

The thought sends a cold chill over my body causing me to shudder. For a moment, I forgot. I believed him. I believed he loved me. But it was only said in the throes of passion. I'm falling for his trap. I feel myself falling for him all over again and I know I need to snap out of it before he hurts me again. Luke rolls off me and onto his side. His large arm wraps around me and pulls me into him. I quickly roll onto my side, facing away from him so he won't see me crying.

"Sugar, what—"

I cut him off before he has a chance to ask. "Thank you." It's all I can think to say. I just want him to leave. I don't want to believe the lies and let him into my heart.

"Thank you?"

"For taking care of that." My voice cracks at the end and I pray he doesn't hear it. My heart aches at how I've just demeaned everything that just happened. Everything I felt between us. But I won't let him think that he's won and that I'll be his toy. I won't let him hurt me again. I can't let him know that I've fallen for him. He'll only use it against me. So instead,

I curl my knees into my stomach and pretend it meant nothing. I pretend I haven't fallen in love with him.

After a moment, I feel him get off the bed and the door closes shortly after. The second the door clicks shut, I question everything. I felt so real. But I just don't trust him.

I cry into the pillow, muffling the sound.

It doesn't matter anyway. I'll be gone soon. I got the story. That's all I really wanted, isn't it? I stare blankly at the wall wishing I could trust my heart. That I could trust his words. I lie in bed, fighting the need to sleep, waiting for him to come back. He doesn't though. He doesn't come back for me.

Soon my eyes are heavy and I fall asleep with a cold ache in my heart.

CHAPTER FOURTEEN

Emma

At some point in the late morning, I slowly roll over in the dim light, expecting to feel Luke in bed. But he's gone. My hand runs along the sheets. They're cold. He never came back. My heart twists in my chest and makes me feel like a fool. What did I really expect?

I gather up the courage to get out of bed. I stretch and groan, feeling how sore my body is. It's only then that I realize I'm starving. The closed door stares back at me and I wonder if Charlotte will be here this morning.

I was prepared to leave them yesterday, but today

feels different. A part of me feels grounded to them, yet still afraid of being used. I don't understand any of what I'm feeling. It's not black and white like words on a page, there's so much muddled gray.

Luke's scent is on the shirt as I slip it on and sigh with remorse. Regret clings to me in more ways than one. I've been using them for my story. It's already written. I nearly sent it to the editor yesterday; I have internet so I could very easily send it even though I'm all too aware I'm not supposed to talk to anyone. So I'd rather be gone and far away from here before I submit it for publication. I don't want to be here when it gets released.

I open up the laptop I've been keeping on my desk and click on my email.

A knock at my door surprises me. I startle, feeling like I've been caught. I close the computer and stuff it back in my bag before calling out, "Come in."

Charlotte walks in, but the bubbly demeanor she possessed the other day is gone. She doesn't even look at me in the eyes. "Luke wanted me to tell you that I'm here if you need anything."

"What?" Did he leave? I don't know what I expected, but the feeling that he's avoiding me sits heavy in my chest.

"He's not feeling well, so he's going to stay away for today." Ice chills my blood as I nod in understanding. "He said you can go out if you want." She subtly scents the air. "Your heat's gone and everything so, you should be fine to do whatever you want." Her voice is laced with disappointment.

"Oh." I don't know what to say. I'd love to go talk to people, to get more for my story. But it feels so wrong. In my heart, I'm already gone. Already back in my empty apartment, typing away and burying myself in my work. I pick at my nails as the tension grows in the room. I've never felt like such a traitor, but she doesn't know the details. She doesn't know everything that happened so she shouldn't judge.

"Is there anything else?" I ask when she doesn't leave.

"Luke said you're leaving. I don't understand." Her words are laced with accusation. My eyes fly to hers. Waiting for her to continue. "Do you just not feel the connection or is it on purpose?"

I part my lips, feeling as though I've betrayed her somehow. Which is ridiculous. "There's more to it than that. There are more important things than a connection."

"Like what? What's more important than love?"

She looks at me with wide, sad eyes, daring me to suggest that love isn't the end all, be all.

"It's not love." She looks at me like I slapped her. I raise my voice and sit up straighter, stopping her from speaking. "It's not love if you're stuck with someone fate picked for you."

"So you don't love him?" Disbelief is written all over her face.

"I want to love him, but I don't trust that it's real. The way we started"—I run my fingers through my hair and force the tears back—"it's just not going to work out. You can't love someone who you don't trust not to hurt you."

"Just give him another chance."

"You don't understand! I gave myself to him and it meant nothing to him!" My emotions are all over the place. I can't contain my hurt any longer.

"I'm sure—"

"No." I raise my voice more than I wanted. "He told me I would beg for him when I was in heat. He knew I'd have to go to him, so he didn't even show me one ounce of respect. I deserve more than that!" The bastard tears leak down my cheeks, and they make me angry more than they do sad. "You're lucky you don't have a mate. You can find someone you love. You're not stuck with whoever fate picked for you."

"But I thought you made up? Couples fight don't they? And he's…he's not the best at expressing himself sometimes. Sometimes people say things they don't mean or—"

"We weren't even a couple yet. He didn't even know me. He still doesn't know me. How could he possibly love me?"

"Why don't you feel that way toward Owen then?"

I'm stunned by her question and fail to come up with a response. It's like a blow to my chest. I just *feel* it with Owen. But it doesn't matter. None of this matters. "I'm leaving anyway so it doesn't matter. I'm sorry I'm going to hurt your Alphas. We just can't stay together. They'll get over it and find someone else."

"They won't."

I wipe the tears away and stalk to the window with my arms crossed. "If I meant anything to him, he would've done more than fucked me last night. He wouldn't have sent you to deal with me." I stare out the window at the forest. "I want to mean more to my partner; Luke can't give me more and Owen will never leave his brother." I turn around and look at Charlotte. "Nothing's going to change that."

"I know he hurt you, but don't you think you've hurt him too?"

"What did I do to him?"

"You denied him."

"I hurt him by not wanting to sleep with someone who treats me like shit? How is that fair?"

"It might not be fair, but it's the truth."

"Well that's what he gets. He doesn't get to treat me like that and then have me bow down to him."

"I wish you'd stay. I wish you'd give him another chance." I can tell the fight in her is nearly gone. Silence lingers between us as I question everything and do all that I can to keep from getting emotional. I'm so sick of feeling emotional.

"Can I ask you one question?"

I nod, waiting for this conversation to be over. My heart just can't take it anymore. I need to get out of here and drown myself in a bottle of wine and forget this ever happened. "Do you feel the connection at all?"

I close my eyes as my heart shatters. I nod my answer and turn back to the window. Letting the pain settle in my chest. I feel a connection to both of them. A deep, powerful spark that makes me feel alive.

She sulks at the door, and I turn away from her and wait to hear it close so I can gather up my shit and get the hell out of here. I gave it a chance and it didn't work. I'm leaving. After a long minute I turn around and snap at Charlotte. "What?"

She's shocked at my anger, and it makes me feel like a bitch. I run my hands across my cheeks, wiping the tears and apologize. "I'm sorry."

"It's okay." She stares at her feet. "I'm just sorry." She starts to leave but pauses in the doorway. "Oh! I forgot to tell you." I pinch the bridge of my nose just wanting to get this over with. "Luke said he's sorry about the story."

"What?" Adrenaline spikes through me, quickening my heart.

"The story. I don't know what he means, but he's sorry." My eyes widen as I register what she's talking about. *He knows about the story.*

"Thank you." The weak words barely register as she closes the door and leaves me standing there.

I walk quickly to my bag and pull out the computer. I barely get half my ass on the bed before I cautiously open it.

I click on my email and wait. An error message pops up. What the fuck? I check Wi-Fi and it's on, but my icons aren't working. I click through applications and nothing. Not a damn thing is opening. That's when I see the desktop. There's a JPEG sitting in the middle of my screen. I click it and open in preview. It's a screenshot of an email sent from me to my editor and boss. My heart plummets and my lips part in shock as I read the message. He destroyed everything I worked for. *Resign.* I didn't fucking resign! That motherfucker! Anger courses through me. He's ended my fucking career!

I search the folder for the manuscript using the search bar, looking in the trash, everywhere on the computer. He fucking deleted it. I jump off the bed and storm to the door. As soon as I open it I slam into a wall of solid muscle. I have to crane my head to look at him and when I do, all my anger dissipates.

"Owen." I barely say his name. "You're back." I'm shocked to see him, but more than that I feel a heavy weight of relief. Not so much so that all of my anger is forgotten.

He strokes my back and kisses the tip of my nose. "What's got you so angry, sweetness?" He noticeably sniffs the air. "You and Luke made up?" My cheeks flush with embarrassment realizing what he's scented. A touch of guilt flows through me, but he's not angry in the least.

"No we haven't, and I want to leave." My voice cracks at the end. "I'm sorry." I can't fucking believe I'm leaving him, but Luke ruining my career is the last straw.

He sucks in a breath as he stares down at me, heartbroken.

I shake my head. "We're just not compatible."

He quietly questions, "You feel nothing for him then?"

"Oh, I feel something. I feel like I want to fucking kill him." I'm barely containing my anger as my blood heats thinking of all the years I've spent getting myself to this point.

"Kill who?" The bastard himself steps into the doorway and strides to the bed like he has no clue why I'd be enraged.

"You!" I scream at him. "How could you ruin my career like that?" Owen grabs my hips, pulling me into him and keeping me from slapping Luke across his face. I stretch an arm out and point as I yell at him. "You have no right going through my things! Do you know what you've done?"

Owen stays quiet behind me, and Luke looks at him, at me, and then back to him. A chill goes through me as I realize they're having a conversation without me. My heart stills at the realization. Owen's going to be so disappointed in me.

Owen's fingertips dig into my hips. "You were a bad, bad girl while I was gone." He bends down and bites my earlobe before whispering, "Weren't you?" The act heats my body and makes my clit throb, while simultaneously startling me.

"I didn't send it." My words come out shaky and I'm not sure if it's because I'm turned on or scared.

"You would have. It was a draft in the email." I stare at Luke, the fucking narc he is, with my lips pressed in a hard line. "Don't worry, sugar, I took care of it for you."

My eyes narrow at him and I hiss, "You sent in my resignation."

He nods his head and smirks like a cocky bastard. "I did."

"I'm not resigning!"

"You already did."

"I don't want to quit!"

"You can find a job here that won't end with us having to go up against the Authority." He's fucking insane if he thinks I'm going to be staying here. And I'm sure as shit not going to settle on another job when what I want to do is just within my reach.

"They deserve to know the truth!" I hear the passion in my voice. I've worked so hard and come so far to try to unite us as a species. And now it's being ripped away from me by someone who claims he loves me.

"That's not up to us." He looks slightly remorseful, but it doesn't stop my anger.

"Fuck you!"

"Oh sugar, you're going to be fucking me." And there's the cocky prick I can't fucking stand.

I scream at him so loud that my throat burns. "This is why you'll never be my mate!"

That gets him moving. He storms over with heat in his eyes and stands right in front of me so my body is pressed between the two of them. "I'm your mate, sugar; you're going to have to deal with that."

I gather up the last bit of courage and sneer. "I'm leaving." I turn in the confined space and look up at Owen. "I want to go home." Owen looks between the two of us but doesn't speak. "You said you'd take me home." My voice loses its strength and cracks. "You promised."

"You are home." I clench my teeth at Luke's words but refuse to turn around and acknowledge him. "You're staying here."

"You can't hold me captive!" Blood rushes in my ears as I feel Owen's grip on me tighten. I realize how wrong I am. They could easily keep me here for as long as they wanted. I'm helpless and at their mercy. "You wouldn't if you loved me," I whisper in the air surrounding us, but already feel defeated. Tears brim my eyes and my body trembles. I can't stay here. This is all too much too soon. None of this was my choice. None of it.

"Don't cry sweetness. I promised I'd—"

"She's my mate too!" Luke yells, interrupting Owen. "And I'm *not* letting her leave!"

"Would you really have us treat our mate this way?" Owen seethes through clenched teeth.

"She's lying." Luke's hand grabs my waist, right above Owen's hands on my hip, and he leans into me so that his breath tickles the shell of my ear. "You keep denying it, but I know you feel this. I know you felt it last night and I'm not going to let you run from it."

I look him dead in the eyes and tell him, "You're an asshole."

"That may be true, but I'm also right. I know you love me, and you know I love you too."

I turn in their grasp and slam my fist on his hard chest as I speak without thinking. "I hate you."

His hands leave me, and I instantly miss his touch. "How did I hurt you so fucking bad?"

"You treat me like I'm expected to just part my legs for you!" Tears fall as I hysterically yell at him, my back to Owen's solid chest. "You don't love me!"

"Don't tell me I don't love you!" He tries to interrupt me, but I continue, yelling over him.

"You're stuck with me!" My face heats and reddens with anger. "You don't want me as a mate!"

"You're right! I didn't want a human for a mate!" His harsh words silence me. I fucking knew it. "But that doesn't mean I don't love you." I shake my head, denying his words. "You can deny me all you want, sugar, but that doesn't make it any less true. I gave you everything that I had last night and you shut me out." His voice raises. "You used me."

"I didn't use you!" My shoulders hunch and I lower my gaze. "I'm just protecting myself."

"From what?" he asks as though he can fix it. How can he be so blind?

"From you!"

He throws his hands up in exasperation, looking at me as though I'm the one who's crazy. "I said I'm sorry!"

"You don't mean it." I spit the words out and push against Owen, trying to break from his hold, but he doesn't let go. I can't deal with this right now.

"You just want to hate me." Luke stalks back toward me. "Is that it? Will this be easier for you if you have a real reason to hate me?"

I continue to struggle against Owen, but he doesn't let up his grip. I sneer back at Luke. "I don't trust you."

"You'll learn to trust me." His tone changes to plead with me and it breaks down my walls. "Give us time. I know you feel it. What I felt last night was real. I know you felt it." His eyes plead with me, but I can't admit it.

"Tell me you feel nothing for me then." He takes my chin in his hand, the contact calms me and forces me to stare into his eyes. "Tell me I'm nothing to you." His sad, softly spoken words crack and his pain resonates through me.

My mouth opens, but I look away. His hand tilts my chin again, forcing my eyes to meet his. I pull in a tortured breath and close my eyes.

"Look at me. Look at me and tell me what you really feel."

"You're going to hurt me." Tears fall down my face. I know he's going to hurt me.

"I promise I won't. I know I was an asshole, but I promise I'll make it up to you. I'll spend every day on my knees making it up to you."

I hesitate to say the truth. To tell him I love him. If this is real, then I'd be at his mercy for the rest of my life. He could hurt me. He already has and he could do it again. It would destroy me to have him treat me like that ever again. He rests his forehead against mine. "I love you, Emma." He kisses my lips, pouring his passion and devotion into the tender touch. "I'll spend my life loving you."

My hands grip his shoulders as I cry into his chest. "I love you, Luke." A strangled sob leaves me. "Please don't hurt me." Owen finally lets go of me and I fall into Luke's chest.

"Never baby. I'll never hurt you again."

His strong hands run up and down my back as I nuzzle into his broad chest. My heart flutters and my chest warms at his affection. I sigh heavily into his chest, trying to calm my breathing and take in this revelation. I lean back to look at Luke, my Alpha, my mate.

His eyes shine with sincerity. "You believe me now, sugar? I mean every word. Please believe me."

I nod, feeling that warmth in my chest flow through my entire body.

"Now what's this about my mate being naughty?" Owen's hard voice in my ear makes me shiver as my heart stills. I suck a breath in; I don't know what to expect, but I know he must be pissed.

"I want this to be good for her Owen." Luke speaks easily over my head. "It's taken care of anyway."

I shift uncomfortably. I don't know what to think about him ending my career. I worked so fucking hard. But now that I'm here. Now that I'm staying…

"Don't worry, we'll find something for you that you'll love, and the Authority, once they are told of our mating, will smooth everything over and find you a worthy position." Luke answers my unasked question. I know the Authority has power in the industry. More questions fill my mind, but they're silenced by my mate.

Owen's hand curls around the nape of my neck and leans in to whisper in my ear, "You're very lucky that Luke saved your ass, sweetness." His sexy voice holds a threat that heats my core.

Both of my mates lean in and kiss my neck on either side. Licking, nipping, and leaving open-mouthed kisses. My pussy clenches as their hands roam my body; I'm not sure whose hands are where, but it doesn't matter. It overwhelms my senses and makes me feel just as needy as I did when I was in heat.

Luke pulls away to look at me, his eyes glowing with desire. "Speaking of that ass." His eyes leave mine to look at Owen. "You better take it right now or I am."

My eyes widen. "I've—" I can hardly breathe at the thought. "I've never done that."

"Good. Then I don't have to kill anyone." Luke's low chuckle in response to Owen's flat statement makes me weak in the knees. It's light between us and with my guard down, the pull to him is undeniable. "You love me," he says teasingly, and the warmth grows between us. "You love me," he repeats, and I swallow thickly.

"I do."

Luke grabs me up by my ass, squeezing both cheeks before tossing me onto the bed. I gasp as I bounce on the mattress. Before I've had time to right myself, Luke cages me in, primal lust in his eyes. His nose brushes against mine and I don't miss the spark in his eyes. All the air in my lungs leaves me as he lowers his body on me, staring at me like a wolf does his prey. His hands play with the hem of my shirt. "You won't be needing this." He grips my shirt and tears it in half, exposing my body to him. My chest rises and falls heavily, unable to move away as his eyes devour my body. "We need to practice claiming you."

Suddenly, he grabs my hips and rolls over, taking me with him so that he's on his back as I straddle him. My hands fly to his hard, muscular chest for balance. His hand grabs the nape of my neck and pulls me toward him, crashing his lips with mine. He nips my lower lip and as I open my mouth to gasp, his tongue invades my mouth, dancing with mine in a hot kiss of passion.

I don't even hear Owen until he's on the bed behind me with his fingers tickling the sides of my thighs as they travel to my panty line. "You don't need these either, sweetness." His thick fingers tear the cotton easily.

I breathe in short, shallow breaths as I realize what's going to happen. My heart quickens and my blood heats. I rock my pussy into Luke's hard cock and rub my throbbing clit against him. Luke groans. "That's right, sugar, use me. I fucking love it when you use me like this." His hand splays on my back and pulls my chest to his.

I hear Owen open a bottle and I crane my neck to watch him behind me. He gently pets my back while stroking his dick, shining with lube. "Don't worry, just relax." My eyes widen as I imagine his massive dick in my ass. No fucking way that's going to fit. I part my lips as my anxiety begs me to object, but a moan is what comes out as Luke cups my pussy and rubs his palm against my clit.

"We've got you, sugar. Let us make you feel good." He leans in and sucks my nipple into his mouth and moans around it as he rocks his dick into my heat. "I'm gonna love watching your tits bounce while I fuck you."

"And I get to make this ass jiggle." Owen's hand comes down hard on my ass cheek, making it spike with a hint of pain and desire. I clench my pussy in heated anticipation.

"At the same time?" I'm surprised by the breathy lust coating my words.

Owen kisses my neck and nips my ear. "Is that what you want?"

Even though my heart races, I don't hesitate to answer as my head rolls back, exposing my throat for Luke to suckle. "Yes."

I whimper into the crook of Luke's neck as Owen stretches me. It's more foreign than painful.

"Push back baby." I do as Owen says and moan as the heated sensation sends a wave of arousal through me. Luke kisses my shoulder and rubs my throbbing clit. I feel on the verge of shattering as they both kiss, lick, and rub my sensitized body. My heart goes into overdrive and a wildfire consumes me as both of them push slowly into me at the same time. Luke pulls my trembling body down as Owen pushes more and more of him into me. Luke's fully seated dick stretches my walls, causing a hint of pain that only adds to my pleasure. I groan as Owen pushes deeper.

"Relax, sugar." One of them rubs my clit as they both kiss and suckle my shoulders until Owen takes me completely. It's almost too much. *So full, so hot.* My body hums with pleasure so close to the tilt of pain, yet somehow I'm still overwhelmed with need.

Owen's chest pushes my body tighter against Luke as his teeth scrape the tender skin of my neck. "This side's mine."

Luke nips the other side. "My mark will go here."

Their confidence in their possession of me, combined with the intensity of our connection, makes my body weak with a primitive need.

"Please," I beg them as my head goes light with lust. I need my release. They take me at the same time, thrusting in and out of me, stretching and filling me only to leave me empty and needing more. My fingernails dig into Luke's shoulders as I bite his neck in an attempt to muffle my screams.

"Fuck yes! Bite me." He pounds harder and faster into me. "Mark me as yours." I moan louder into his neck as every nerve ending in my body fires at full force, taking me on a high I've never experienced in my life. Owen's blunt nails dig into the flesh of my hips as he pumps into my ass with harder strokes. Every thrust makes my body vibrate with pleasure. Owen growls and Luke snarls, each buried deep inside of me as I scream out my orgasm, burning my throat and leaving my lungs with no air.

I fall on Luke's chest, breathless, sated, and feeling complete in every way. They've stripped me, fucked me, and claimed me as theirs. My Alphas.

EPILOGUE

I CAN'T STOP LICKING MY MARK ON HER NECK. Even as she sleeps soundly between us, I have to lean in and lick it again. As I lean back to admire the red mark from my bite, Owen leans in and licks his own mark, making our mate roll on her side and wiggle her ass closer to my dick. I expect my wolf to snarl at his claim on her, but he hardly responds, content and at peace that our mate allowed us to claim her tonight. It's been three days since she stopped holding back and refusing to believe I love her, and each day is better than the last.

Our bond is one thing, my love for her another.

She has as much control over the bond as I do, but my love for her…that's something neither of us can control or deny. I love her more than anything.

"Do you smell that?" I smile at Owen's question knowing exactly what he's talking about.

"If this one's yours, I get her all to myself next heat."

He laughs at my response. "Selfish prick." A huff of a laugh leaves me as I push the hair from her face. To think I almost let her fool me into thinking I meant nothing to her. My heart clenches.

"We need to go see Jude." My eyes raise from our resting mate to my brother, not liking his tone.

"Why's that?" His stern expression leaves me with a tension I don't like.

"The coven will need us, and we will need the Shadow Falls pack on our side."

"Our side of what?"

Owen swallows thickly. "A faction is growing, wanting to challenge the Authority."

I suppress my growl, only to prevent the noise from waking our mate. I push my words through clenched teeth. "We will not go against the Authority." How could he possibly think that would be acceptable? With our mate at our side, I won't let any danger come to her.

"I don't want to and neither do they, but a rebellion

has started." I look down at our mate, listening to my brother as his words hit me with a force that has my wolf snarling with rage. "Anyone not on their side is seen as an enemy."

"Who would be stupid enough to challenge the Authority? To challenge the covens? They dare to challenge us?"

"A select few." I sit back against the headboard, feeling confident that this won't be an issue.

"Luke"—my eyes find his—"the dragons are on their side." My heart stops and my blood runs cold.

"Are you sure?" No one has heard from the dragons in nearly a hundred years. He nods his head, resigned to the idea of going to war. I clench my fists, not wanting to be a part of anything that could hurt our mate.

"You're right." I nod my head. "We'll need the numbers." My body chills as my eyes find his. "You think it will mean war?"

His eyes fall to our sleeping mate. "I hope that's not the case, but whether or not there will be war, the dragons are coming. Something brought them out, and according to the coven, it involves a mate."

ABOUT THE AUTHOR

Thank you so much for reading my romances. I'm just a stay at home mom and avid reader turned author and I couldn't be happier.

I hope you love my books as much as I do!

More by Willow Winters
www.WillowWintersWrites.com/books